BEAU

CINDERMAMA BOOK 3

INES JOHNSON

THOSE JOHNSON GIRLS

Edited by Dragonfly Editing
Cover design by Yocla Designs

Manufactured in the United States of America
First Edition March 2017

1
———

Beau wrenched herself awake and out from the dark tendrils of sleep. Her eyes slammed open to the glaring twilight. Her arms flew out to ward off the cloying shadows. Her chest heaved in shallow pants and her fingers curled around the empty air. Her eyes took long to adjust to the darkness that shone bright in the room.

Bile on her tongue mixed with the metallic tint of iron. She reached her cold, shaking fingers to her lip. They came away wet. She eyed the contrast of the dark blood on her pale fingertips, and then glanced up at her surroundings.

Nothing looked familiar.

Where was she?

She took a deep breath, but her tight chest protested, only allowing one tiny puff of air at a time through its constricted channels. It left her dizzy as the four walls crushed in on her with the ever-growing darkness.

This was wrong, her mind whispered. Her restless legs tingled; eager to get up and run. Her churning stomach insisted she wasn't supposed to be here in this place; this cold, dark place.

A hand snaked out to grab at her. She wrenched away from it, skittering to the far side of the bed.

Bed? She was in a bed?

"Beau?" A deep voice, muffled with sleep, called out into the night. "Baby, it's me."

Who?

The voice sounded irritated, annoyed. Beau wasn't certain she wanted to get any closer to the owner of the voice. She peered down into the darkness until the face attached to the voice came into view. She couldn't make out the man's features. His face was shrouded in the shadows that surrounded them both. But there was something familiar about him.

He reached out again. This time he caught her. His fingertips left cold spots on the underside of her wrist, causing her pulse to jump. She stared down at the cold spots as her pulse kicked at his thumb.

She balled her hand into a fist, meeting another cold shock. It was a piece of metal. A band; a thin golden band. Her thumb snaked between her middle and fourth finger and met the sharp point of a stone.

"It's okay, baby." The words came as though from a record player that had worn out this particular song. "You had the nightmare again."

Nightmare? Had she had a nightmare? She didn't remember any pictures in her mind, only darkness. She'd been lost inside of darkness. Darkness from all around her; in her head, and now in reality.

She'd been looking for something? Or maybe for someone? She wasn't sure? It had been so dark. She shivered at the memory of it. Opening her eyes, she shivered again at the reality of it.

"You're home, baby," he said.

Beau looked around the dark room. This was her room, in her home. But why would she have a room so dark if she hated the darkness? Even with her eyes open, she felt the dense shadows crushing her still.

"You're with me," he said.

That sounded right. She moved closer to the voice, to him.

She knew this man, had known him for much of her life. She'd known him back during the time when sleep came quietly and peacefully to her. When dreams had whispered secrets to her. When waking had been a delight. Before nightmares of darkness kept her from her dreams and stole a little piece of her soul every time she closed her eyes.

"Everything's fine." The man with the familiar voice sighed heavily. The bed creaked as he turned over onto his other side. "Go back to sleep." He settled into the sheets. Within a minute, he was softly snoring.

Beau took another deep breath. Her chest now calm enough to allow clear passage for enough air to fill her lungs. Her heart slowed. Her stomach settled.

She closed her eyes, but the darkness waiting beneath her lashes crawled over her eyelids. It taunted her like a schoolyard bully, goading her to try and escape its wrath. She opened her eyes, but the shadows rang loud from their place in the corners of the room. She swore she heard them mocking her.

She slid closer to the man on the far side of the bed, seeking out his warmth. She ran her hands over his strong bicep.

He jerked away from her. "Babe, I've got a busy day tomorrow."

He turned to her, and gave her a quick kiss at the corner

of her mouth. Then he turned away, scooting to the edge of his side of the bed. He gave her his back again.

Beau scooted away from him, back to her side of the mattress, which was colder, darker. She shoved the fear down. She pushed away thoughts of being in the wrong place. This was exactly where she was supposed to be. Lying beside the man of her dreams, in the house of her dreams, with the life of her dreams.

She had everything she'd ever dreamed of, and when she woke in the morning it would all be here to greet her. She pulled the covers up to her chin, then over her eyes.

She willed herself to sleep. But the darkness hovered, waiting to make its next attack.

Beau decided to stop fighting. She tossed off the covers and got up to greet the day, even though it was still the dead of the night.

2

———————

"Green means go, Mommy."

Beau blinked her eyes awake. She jerked in the driver's seat at the blare of the horn behind her telling her to move forward. She'd closed her eyes for a split second while being stopped at a stoplight on a residential street. At least, she hoped it had only been for a split second.

"Are we gonna be late again, Mommy?" In the mommy-mirror Beau's five-year old daughter, Flora, clutched at her pink, Disney princess backpack. Blue-gray eyes blinked back, moistened from anxious tears. The precious girl pulled a lock of jet-black hair into her mouth.

"No, sweetie," Beau soothed, flicking her own light-gray eyes up to the car's rear mirror. She pushed a lock of her own jet black hair behind her ear. "We're almost there."

Beau pulled her lower lip into her mouth at the small fib. They were almost to the children's school, relative to where they were five minutes ago. She took her foot off the brake and tapped the gas. Turning one-handed into the next lane, she took the opportunity to take a healthy gulp of her second cup of coffee.

The dark roast sent a liquid shot of adrenalin into her blood stream. Unfortunately, the caffeine from her first cup still lingered in her veins and the newest sip from her second cup fizzled on impact. The insomnia was killing her. She had to keep alert. If not for herself, then for the precious cargo she carried in the backseat.

"Mommy, I said I wanted a strawberry cereal bar." A face identical to Flora's, but with cropped curls, filled the mommy-mirror. Her son, Faun, screwed his face at the blueberry cereal bar.

The children were having backseat breakfast again, because Beau missed her alarm clock. After waking in the middle of the night, she'd putzed around the house, finally venturing into her home office, which was a floor away from her bedroom. She'd picked up a file from work and had begun making notes. She didn't remember exactly when she'd closed her eyes.

The next time she opened them was to the slam of the front door, which had been her husband, Philip, leaving for the gym. He couldn't start his day without a good workout. Back in the home office, Beau had taken one look at the computer's clock and realized she and the children would be late starting their own day, which meant she didn't have time to make them a healthy breakfast from scratch.

"Faunie, you already ate yours."

"But Flo has one now," Faun kicked the back of the driver's seat.

Beau glanced at Flora. The little girl took the lock of hair out of her mouth and pulled it over her shut eyes. The unopened cereal bar lay on her lap.

"I want another one," whined Faun.

"Here," Flora handed hers to her brother. "You can have mine. I don't want it."

Faun smacked the food away. "I don't want yours. I want my own."

Flora tried again to hand the unopened bar to her brother, but he pitched an even bigger fit, kicking up a storm that Beau felt along her spine.

"Flo, if he doesn't want it then stop teasing him," Beau admonished. The last thing she needed this morning was her son to have one of his meltdowns. When he got riled up it was almost impossible to calm him down.

Everyone told her that having twins was a full time job in and of itself. Not only did Beau have two children whom she loved, she also had a full-time job that was her life's passion. A job she would be late for, if she didn't get it into gear and get the kids to school on time.

Finally, she rounded the corner to Parish Academy with a moment to spare before the first bell. It was a straight path to the front of the school, as the drop off lane was empty of cars. The majority of parents had already kissed their kids and ridden off to make it to work on time. Only the moms of the shame-squad lingered, chatting in their Lulelemons and designer jeans. Since Beau couldn't escape the late-walk-of-shame, she pasted on a bright smile as she put the car in park and hopped out to unload her children.

"Hi, ladies," she sing-songed.

"Hi, Isabeau," rang a chorus of falsettos.

"What I wouldn't give to have the luxury of sleeping in on a school day," one voice broke off from the pack.

It was Chantelle, the leader of the pack. The dark-skinned woman wore a size zero yoga pants with a matching crop top that hinted at a flat, stretch-mark-less belly. Her artfully messy ponytail swished across her shoulder blades and her smoky-shadowed eyes cast shade at Beau.

Beau couldn't pass her puffy, encircled eyes off as a new makeup craze. She would love the luxury of sleeping in herself. She couldn't remember the last time she'd slept longer than a stolen nap during the day.

"Traffic was a nightmare," Beau offered as an excuse.

They all knew she only lived a couple of miles from the elite private school. They all lived in the same neighborhood. Most of them jogged here with their tricked-out jogging strollers, with designer tennis skirts hugging their perky asses. Beau didn't have time for jogging. She also didn't have time for small talk in the kiss-and-ride lane.

She unbuckled the twins and they hopped out of the car. Faun barely spared his mother a glance as she leaned down to kiss him goodbye. He ducked and sprinted for his teacher, Mrs. Knighting, giving the older woman a hug.

Mrs. Knighting straightened and gave Beau an enthusiastic wave. Beau had known Mrs. Knighting when her gray hair was still a lush brown and her name was Ms. Clark. Twenty years ago, the night after her first day of Kindergarten, Beau had seen Ms. Clark in a dream. She hadn't understood what it meant that her teacher and the school crossing guard were holding hands as they walked in a meadow. Mr. Knighting had held Beau's hand that morning when she'd crossed the street to school. The next morning Beau told Ms. Clark about the dream. That afternoon Beau saw the two adults talking. Within the year they were married.

Flora waited patiently for her mother to lean down and kiss her forehead. "Love you, Mommy," she said, before skipping off to join her brother.

Beau took a moment she didn't have to watch the two

children disappear into the school with their teacher. They were the last two children to do so. Then she turned to head back to her car, but she knew better. The Mom Squad swarmed on her.

"We've been looking for some parents to come and talk with the children next week for Career Day." Chantelle's ponytail swished hypnotically as she sized up Beau.

"Oh, I..." Beau fell under the spell of the dark mane and didn't get an excuse out in time.

"We have a lot of fathers coming in, but not many women work outside of the home. You're one of the few." Lindsey stood at Chantelle's side, coordinated from her jean belt to her earrings, to her nail polish. Beau wondered what time the woman got up in the morning to affect such a look?

"We were hoping you'd get more involved this year, like you promised." Kathryn pulled up on Beau's other side. They'd effectively boxed her in. There was no way to escape.

They'd not only boxed her in physically, they also cut her at her Achilles' heel. Beau came from money; lots of money. She never wanted to be accused of being entitled — even though just about every woman whose kids were enrolled in this prestigious and expensive private school was connected to money and rarely worked a day in their lives.

Three pairs of eyes regarded her, looking down on her even though she had a couple of inches, and a few more zeros in a trust fund, on each of them. Chantelle's ponytail swished back and forth in anticipation of Beau squirming out of yet another school function, as she'd done in the past.

It wasn't that Beau didn't want to help out. She just didn't have the time to. Her philanthropic enterprise, aimed at educating girls in the Middle East so they'd have options other than arranged marriages, and rescuing boys taken to soldier wars in Africa, always interfered with the involvement in this high-priced, exclusive, private, primary school.

Chantelle's gaze broke from Beau's. She cocked her head, ponytail swishing like a lion scenting easy prey. "Uh oh, look out. Charity case incoming."

Beau turned to see an old-school Chevy pull up. The muffler grunted as the car pulled to a stop. A woman Beau didn't recognize hopped out of the car. She wore loose-fitting jeans and a sweatshirt with a stain at the collar.

The woman opened the car door with a squeak of metal and three kids paraded out. It was a Benneton of Color ad. One child was Asian, another black, and a third... Beau couldn't quite distinguish the third child's ethnicity, but he had pale-skin and European features.

"They're here on scholarship." Chantelle crossed her brown arms beneath her perky breasts. "The board is trying to get into Affirmative Action."

"I heard her husband left her after the second child came out Asian," said Lindsey.

The woman in question had skin the color of milk with a teaspoon tipped with chocolate, and bright orange-red hair. The combination of her skin and hair was stunning. Beau wondered if the woman was an albino.

The mom opened her arms and each child came willingly into her embrace before heading into the building. When the red-head straightened and turned, her face did not read excitement at the prospect of a face-off with the Mom Squad. In fact, she tried to side step them altogether.

Beau let out a small sigh for the woman. That move never worked, she wanted to tell the newcomer. Best to just face the pack head on and soldier through.

"Duchess," Chantelle sing-songed across the lot. She leaned into Beau and whispered, "Can you believe that name?"

Duchess didn't venture too close. "Hello, everyone. It's good to see you all."

Chantelle stepped in front of her, cutting off Duchess' exit. "You know that part of enrollment in Parish Academy is that every family has to do community service hours. We were hoping you could come in next week for Career Day. You're one of the only working moms in the school. And we want to show the little girls that there are a few other options than an MRS degree."

Duchess cocked her head like a bird, unsure if the landing was safe. "I don't know. I work during school hours." Duchess took another step towards her car.

"Oh, it won't take much time at all. You'd be speaking along with Isabeau, here."

Duchess took one look at Beau in her pressed suit and pumps and winced. For all of her wealth and popularity Beau had never been a mean girl. She broke off from the herd and extended her hand to Duchess.

"I'm pleased to meet you," Beau said. "I think it would be fun to speak with the kids, and I'd love if we did it together."

Duchess blinked at Beau's genuine smile. Then she took her hand. Duchess' grip wasn't firm, but it was warm.

"You headed in to work?" Beau asked.

Duchess nodded.

"Me, too." Beau commandeered them towards their cars and out of the way of the Mom Squad.

"Thanks," said Duchess.

"No, thank you. I really do have a meeting to get to. They would've kept me there all day. I'm Beau, by the way."

Duchess cocked her head to the other side in the same bird-like motion. "Yes, I know."

Right, Chantelle had said her name. "Well, Duchess, maybe we could get together sometime on a weekend to get to know each other?"

"You want to hang out?" she said. "With me?" She pointed her thumb to her chest. It landed at the stain on her shirt.

"Sure," said Beau. "Maybe make a play date out of it with the kids?"

"Yeah... okay." Duchess' smile was wobbly with uncertainty, but it wasn't fake.

They exchanged numbers and then the two women hopped into their cars and left the school, and the Mom Squad, behind.

Twenty minutes later, and with truly horrific rush hour traffic, Beau pulled up to her office. The Rosen Foundation was a small non-profit, only three years old. Unlike the Charmayne Foundation run by Beau's family, which focused on the sick and the needy, the Rosen Foundation focused its efforts specifically on children.

The office occupied what used to be a flower shop in the market district of Saint Anne's parish. The shop had belonged to Mr. Matthews. Mr. Matthews had been a widower when he bought the shop. One night in high school, Beau had seen him arranging black and white flowers for her brother's music teacher.

By this time Beau had come to understand her gift, and was sure to tell the music teacher about the flower shop. The flowers at the wedding were beautiful. Beau's brother, Guy, never forgave her for butting into the life of his favorite teacher, who became pregnant within a year and never went back to teaching after the first, then second, and third child was born.

The converted flower shop was mainly one large room with a small office in the back, next to the bathroom. Beau could have run the organization from the Charmayne offices free rent, but Philip had insisted they have their own space and their own identity.

The business didn't take up too much space, as most of the work was done on the phone, calling up potential donors; and at social events, networking with wealthy socialites and philanthropic business professionals whose consciences were eager to give back. Beau and Philip shared the small back office, but Beau spent most of her time in the main room with her small staff. The staff consisted of college interns; mainly poli-sci majors. Interns worked for free in exchange for college credit. Unfortunately, Beau's interns had the bad habit of acing the internship class and then moving on, leaving her with the task of training a new batch every few months.

The office was empty at eight in the morning, when most of the interns were hitting their snooze buttons. Beau set her bag down on one of the empty cubicles and walked back to the office. Philip stood at the window of his office in a tailored suit.

Beau halted in her stride. The sight of him standing there in that particular pose, in a suit... it called to mind a dream she'd had of him when she was in college. That dream had changed her life.

Magic ran in Beau's family. Her mother had seen her father coming a mile away, when he'd glowed bright, before her eyes. Beau and her brother didn't get the Charmayne gift of seeing golden auras around their true love. Their gifts were different. Her brother Guy saw gold around people with talent. Beau didn't see any gold. In fact, she didn't see anything at all any more. Her gift had been short-lived. But it didn't matter. It had served its purpose and brought her the man of her dreams.

Beau allowed herself a moment to admire the man she'd pledged to spend her life with. She got her feet moving again, eager to feel the warm, reality of him with her hands.

"There you are," he turned with an exasperated look when he saw her. "You're late. I had to entertain Stefan Paulson for the last twenty minutes."

The office they shared also doubled as a conference room. Meeting Mr. Paulson was the first thing on her long to-do list today, and she was thankful to her husband for taking care of that task.

"Thank you for doing that. How much is he in for?" she asked, leaning against the solid oak desk that Philip insisted they needed to impress big donors.

"How should I know?" Philip coordinated a shrug and a frown. "That's your job, to work with the small businessmen."

Stefan Paulson was a local dentist. His mother was origi-nally from Sudan, but had married an American man when she relocated to the States. Dr. Paulson had no ties to his mother's homeland, but he felt pulled to do something about the violence occuring in that land, especially the theft of bright, young boys who were then turned into killing machines to feed an endless war.

"He came with his checkbook," she said. "All you had to do was offer him a pen. What did you talk about for twenty minutes?"

"Sports." Philip barely spared her a glance as he shoved items into his golf bag. "He'll be back later this afternoon to speak with you."

Beau stifled a sigh. There went her early escape from work to get to the grocery store before she had to pick the kids up from school. The day crowded in on her like the darkness of her dream last night. What she wouldn't give for a day's rest. Instead, she'd be brewing a third cup of coffee in less than two hours.

"You also need to look over some documents from the IRS about our non-profit status," Philip grabbed his cell phone and tapped a few keys. "Something about new guidelines with phone calls. I don't know? You take a look."

Beau looked down at the IRS documents she had to view. Besides that, she had a mountain of paperwork to go through on her desk. Then she had a ton of calls to make. Not to mention she'd have to spare some time to think about what she'd say for Career Day next week. Which reminded her about her empty fridge. It looked like it would be another take-out night for the Rosen family.

"Anyway, your tardiness is going to make me late," he said.

"Late for what? What's on your agenda today?" she asked as Philip struggled with his briefcase. There were very few documents in the case's belly.

"I'm headed to the golf course. I have that meeting with a new consultant."

"Consultant?"

"Yeah. Yohance Stanley. I told you about him. He's perfected this new technique to help fundraise; it saves tons of money."

Philip poked at the latch on the case, it refused to close. He smacked at it, then huffed when it still refused to close. Beau reached for the case and took it from his grasp. The last thing she needed this morning was her husband to have one of his meltdowns. When he got riled up it was almost impossible to calm him down.

Beau lined the latch up and it snapped closed. Philip sighed. He pulled her close and kissed her temple. Beau relaxed into his arms.

"Listen baby, I know how hard you work to get the money in. But we should be thinking of working smarter and not harder. I'm going to hear Mr. Stanley out, see if we can use any of his techniques to lighten the load around here."

He kissed her temple again, and then released her. She knew she should ask Philip to schedule a meeting so they could both hear this consultant out, but the thought of another thing added to her list made her bones weary. Instead, she waved to Philip as he hefted his golf bag over his shoulder and headed out the door.

She'd just sat down at the expensive desk and begun mentally organizing her to-do list, when she realized he'd left his brief case behind. It was too late to go after him. She knew he'd call her if he needed anything. She pushed the light case aside and got down to work.

3

"Are you enjoying your meal?" Darrell asked, as the smell of butter and sea filled the air.

His date's lobster was almost as big as her head. She held a tiny fork in one hand and a steak knife in the other. She dug in, but the crustacean fought back, slipping first to one side of the buttery dish then to the other as she tried to reel it in with her utensils.

"I've never had lobster before," she said.

Darrell sat back and watched the show. It looked like he would get lucky tonight. He'd read up online about dating and dishes. A psychologist compiled a study that gave the personality traits of individuals based on what they ordered on a date. Ordering meat and potatoes meant that a person was steady, dependable, and enjoyed the comforts of home. Looking down at his plate, Darrell could confirm the diagnosis.

When a woman ordered an expensive dish like a lobster, which was the most expensive dish on the menu, it meant they were wild, adventurous, and up for taking chances. Darrell didn't want to take any chances tonight.

He'd rather the chance be taken a few nights from now. He'd be open to rolling the dice in a couple of weeks, even. The thought of another one-night stand, or a temporary bed-buddy pact did not interest him. He was looking for something more.

Darrell focused on the woman seated across from him. Carla was her name. He'd repeated it to himself exactly twenty-one times. It was scientifically proven that doing something twenty-one times would cause it to become a habit. That would've been the worst thing —to forget someone's name on the first date.

"So Harold—"

"It's Darrell."

"What? Oh, right, Darrell."

Carla shoved her fork up the lobster's tail and plopped the extracted white meat into her mouth. Then she made a face and spit the hunk of meat out. The white blob settled on his plate, right on top of his steak.

Darrell put a hand to his stomach to stop it from roiling.

"Gawb." Carla dabbed her tongue with the linen napkin. Her face screwed up like a toddler who'd just tried baby peas for the first time. "Oh, woub bay por dat cwab."

Darrell picked the mangled bite of lobster off his steak using his napkin. He could admit that lobster was an acquired taste. He called the waiter over.

The mountain of a man made his way over to their table. The waiter's movements were like the parting of the sea. With each step he took, women turned to look behind him at his backside.

Darrell knew that women were biologically predetermined to favor large men. Their lizard brains understood that a large male could protect them best. That a well-filled chest meant he got the best portions of food and she would too. That big men would likely breed big children who would continue their line.

Times had changed since the Mesozoic Era. Changed even further from the hunter gatherer societies. Nerds now ruled the world. If that waiter's cell phone wouldn't turn on, if his computer caught a virus, if his surround-sound stereo went on the fritz, he would have to call someone from Darrell's tribe.

Darrell shoved his glasses up his nose and tilted his head back. He opened his mouth to speak for his date, only to find she'd been caught up in the parting of the seas along with the rest of the women.

"My current dish isn't to my liking." Carla waved her hand above her dismembered lobster. Her fingers waggled in the general direction of Darrell.

"I'm not surprised," said the waiter, his wide back to Darrell. "I didn't think you were the kind of girl who liked bottom feeders."

"Lobster's a little rich for my tastes." Carla flipped her hair over her shoulder and batted her eyelashes. "What do you suggest I try?" Carla ran her tongue over her bottom lip. The waiter followed the movement and his own lips curled.

"Maybe you're the type of girl who needs an aphrodisiac. Try the oysters."

"Oysters are high in zinc, which is great for fertility," said Darrell.

Both Carla and the waiter blinked and frowned down at him.

"I'm on the pill, the patch, and a cervical cap. Nothing is getting fertilized any time soon." Carla turned her attention back to the waiter and winked. "But I'll try the oysters."

The man was absolutely not getting a tip for this shoddy service. Darrell's water glass was empty. He'd asked for a steak knife ten minutes ago. And to top it off, the man was hitting on his date. But what did he expect?

Darrell had been to a number of speed dating events in the past couple of months. To his shock, he learned that a lot of women were out looking for short-term hookups, not a lasting relationship. Apparently, today's workingwoman didn't have time to forge relationships. He'd heard a number of women say so, on more than one occasion.

Today's woman had needs and went out to bars and clubs and speed dating events to get those needs met. Darrell had learned the hard way that there was no require-ment for breakfast in the morning, or even cuddling at night. Today's meat market was no longer full of female lambs meant for slaughter. Male lambs were often on the block as just a side dish.

He'd met Carla the other day at one such event. He'd read her dating profile on the lock-shaped card that hung around her neck. His profile data was listed on a key-shaped card. He admitted the whole scenario was a bit phallic, but it saved time. Their cards had told him they had a lot in common. Commonality, he believed, was the foundation of any good relationship.

"So, Carla," he began. "I remember from your profile that you're a nursing student."

Carla shook her head. "That was, like, forever ago. I dropped out two years ago."

"Oh?" Darrell rubbed at his chin. "Well, what do you do now?"

"I work for the cable company."

"You're in communications?" He worked with people too, both as a profession and in his spare time.

Carla shook her head. "Debt collection."

They were silent for a moment. Both glancing around the restaurant. Carla had suggested they go out for an early dinner. At the time, Darrell had thought she was being cautious to not be out late with a man she didn't know. Now he wondered if he was just the warm up act and the main show would later take the stage. Carla looked at the curtain where the wait staff passed through. Darrell looked at the exit sign in the corner.

"You're a doctor, right?" Carla's eyes held a spark of interest when they turned back to him.

One thing Darrell knew he had going for him was his credentials. Just as jocks grew up to be in the service of nerds, women grew out of their infatuations with high school quarterbacks and later aimed for the men whose careers didn't have them bashing into one another and running in circles. "I am. I'm a chiropractor."

Her eyebrows drew together. "Is that a real doctor?"

Darrell kept his grimace at bay as he nodded. "I specialize in the spine. You can't get by without a back."

Darrell grinned but Carla looked at him confused. He'd tried that joke out on a number of women at the speed-dating event. Not one of them had laughed. He'd have to retire it from his repertoire.

"So, Carla, what is it you're looking for in a man?"

She parted her lips in a smile that read cynical. "Are we talking in his head or in his pants?"

Darrell choked on his sip of water.

Carla narrowed her eyes at him. "Don't tell me you're one of those romantics? What? You believe in love at first sight?"

Unfortunately, Darrell didn't have the luxury of denying it. He'd seen love at first sight happen. It just so happened that the woman whose attention he had been trying to catch had looked right past him and fallen in love with the friend who had stood beside him.

Darrell cleared his throat. "It's statistically improbable to determine that you'll marry a person based on the first time you see them."

Carla scratched at her eyelid as she frowned at him.

"But it is possible," he conceded. "By a very small margin. I think it's more sound to get to know someone first. To look for things you have in common with each other, before you decide if you'll spend the rest of your life with them."

He waved a hand between the two of them, but Carla wasn't looking at him any longer. She was looking over her shoulder. Darrell saw the approaching waiter with her oyster dish.

"I don't believe in marriage," she said as the waiter placed her new dish before her. "I'm just looking to get laid."

Beside them a child began a tantrum. Darrell looked over to see the neighboring table's empty plates. The mother held up her hand, trying to get the waiter's attention. The waiter had his full attention on Carla's breasts instead.

Darrell had been raised by a single mother. He understood the need for a mother to get out of the house and not cook a meal. When he was a kid, he tried to have dinner ready for his mother as often as he could. Normal gender roles were non-existent in his house. He'd do laundry when necessary. His mother would do the plumbing. They worked together. She had to take on the role of nurturer and father since Darrell's father had chosen to make another family when he was young; a family that didn't include him.

He handed the breadbasket on his table over to the young mom. She made to make a motion to refuse, but when the child's eyes lit, and his crying stopped, she mouthed a 'thank you' at him.

Darrell considered switching tables. But he caught the sparkle of a diamond on the mom's left hand when she reached for the basket. Darrell sighed and turned back to the woman across from him. Unlike the mom, Carla was up for grabs, in more ways than one.

Darrell wanted to find someone. Single life was not for him, though he'd been single most of his thirty years. He'd had a girlfriend here and there. He'd had a few one-night stands and brief trysts over the past year that left him feeling nothing but lonely. Sitting across from Carla, who was busy watching the waiter walk away from their table, Darrell felt that loneliness crush into him. He wanted to be the one chosen for once in his life. Instead of sitting by and bearing it, he did something he was not too proud of.

He reached in his pocket and pulled out his cell phone. He gave Carla an apologetic wince—not that she was paying any attention to him as she dug into her oysters. Darrell turned his attention to the dark screen of his phone. He tapped the blank screen and placed the phone to his ear.

"Hello... Oh, no... Really? Well, of course, I'll be right over." He sighed as he placed the phone back in his pocket. "I'm sorry, Carla but I've got to go. Chiropractic emergency."

"I didn't know there was such a thing," she said, around the food in her mouth.

Darrell pulled out enough cash to cover the bill. Unfortunately, his conscious wouldn't let him exclude the tip. But he only gave ten percent. "It was nice meeting you..."

He hesitated to tack on the customary 'We should do

this again' or 'I'll call you.' They both knew this was the last time they'd ever see each other.

No sooner had Darrell stepped out of the restaurant did he spy, through the window, Carla leave the table and make her way up to the waiter. The two pulled out their phones, smiling carnally at each other.

Love at first sight? The One? True Love?

Those were all pipe dreams. That wasn't love between those two, it was lust. They'd slake each other's needs later tonight and likely be on to the next dish by tomorrow evening.

Darrell wasn't into that. He wanted a partner, someone to share his life with. A woman who was kind, smart, and loyal. Most of all loyal.

One thing he would concede was that Carla and her waiter had it right. The way to find companionship nowadays was through technology. Darrell was a man of science and he would go about finding a woman to share his life with in a scientific manner. No more speed dates where he'd try to gauge a woman's interest in five minutes.

The sun was starting to set as he pulled open his phone and walked to his car. He wasn't going to give up. He was just going to go about this smarter. He tapped a few keys and the dating app downloaded.

The app was like applying for a job. He had to put in his qualifications, accomplishments, and interests. It promised to show him his perfect matches based on algorithms. This was a much simpler, foolproof way to date. And within ten minutes, he already had his first match.

4

Beau reached for her fifth cup of coffee. She smiled as she brought the cup to her lips. The coffee mug was a Wonder Woman cup; starry blue with a red handle. Her mother gave it to her when she was a child.

Gabrielle Charmayne-Rumpel had been a devotee of the Amazonian warrior princess. Growing up during an era when the feminine archetype was under attack by burning bras, Gabrielle had found her ideal in the 70's television show. There was no situation Wonder Woman couldn't handle. No villain she couldn't outwit. No brute she couldn't lasso into submission. Gabrielle had seen the woman she wanted to be in the liberated, strong, unconventional, yet still feminine, woman that Lynda Carter portrayed, and she'd passed these ideals on to her only daughter.

Beau was Amazonian tall with dark tresses and light eyes. She'd been raised to be a strong and liberated, yet still feminine, woman. She was all these things. But try as she might, she never seemed in command of her days.

Two of her interns called in to say they would be late.

One never showed up at all. A huge donor fell through her hands because she hadn't had the time to call and schmooze him before another charity did. She'd never even made it to the new stack of papers Philip had laid on her desk. And then there was her other full-time job waiting to be picked up from the afterschool program, all the way on the other side of town.

Motherhood was harder than the job she spent her days at. She had thirty minutes to make it to the grocery store and then across town to pick up the kids. She had more balls up in the air than she had hands to juggle. If she wasn't careful, everything would come crashing down around her.

"Mrs. Rosen?"

Beau looked up at Judy, her longest and most dependable intern who would, unfortunately, be graduating soon.

"Mr. Paulson is back."

Beau moved one stack of papers over and pulled forth another. A second look at the clock told her that she wouldn't be able to take this meeting with Mr. Paulson, plus get groceries, and get the kids from school on time. Something would have to give.

"Thanks Judy, I'll be out in just a second."

Beau picked up the phone and called for backup.

"Hey, baby." Philip's voice was a rushed whisper. "I can't talk. I'm at the club."

Beau frowned at the phone. "I thought you were golfing with that consultant, what was his name again?"

"Yohance Stanley," said Philip. "I'm with him now. He's interested in taking a look at our organization, but first you're going to need to cut a check for ten thousand."

Beau balked. It wasn't as though they didn't have the money. Well, she had the money. The business didn't.

"Philip, that's incredibly steep."

"It's a steal, Beau. Stanley says 'no' to ninety-percent of the organizations who ask for his services."

"We should at least talk about this more before we cut a check. I haven't had a moment to look up Stanley or his business practices. We should look into this together and meet him together. We are partners, after all."

"Look, they're calling me. I gotta go, babe."

"Wait! Philip?"

"Yeah, babe? What? I'm working here."

"I know, sweetie. But I'm about to meet with Mr. Paulson."

"Okay," he huffed, impatience lacing his voice.

"Which means I won't be able to pick the kids up on time and get dinner on the table. The club is near their school. Can you swing by and get them?"

"Babe, I have no idea how long this meeting is going to last."

"If he's as exclusive as he says, we'll intrigue him by playing hard to get. Besides, these are your children."

The silence on the other end of the phone was crushing. "What's going on here? Are you trying to say I'm a bad father?"

"Philip, I would never say that."

"Because I'm out working, trying to feed my family. If you can't handle all of your responsibilities—"

"Wait a minute. That's not fair."

"Did I call you up asking you to come down here? No, I didn't. I took it upon myself to seek out someone who could make your life easier."

Philip was getting riled up. He was almost impossible to calm down when he got upset, and she didn't want him to cause a scene in the country club.

"You're the one who wanted to be a working mother," he huffed. "You could've stayed home with the kids."

That had been the plan; for Beau to stop working at Charmayne Foundation and stay home with the twins. Shortly after she and Philip were married, and she was still in her first trimester, Philip had gone to work with his father. Unfortunately, things didn't work out there because, well, Philip and his father were too alike, and two cooks in the kitchen was a recipe for disaster.

So, Philip's father gave him a loan and sent his son off to start his own company. That company never got off the ground because something or other about not filing the right permits by the deadlines. Beau had never gotten a clear explanation out of her demoralized husband. In her final trimester, and large with the twins, she came to learn that he'd spent the majority of those funds on their new home and filling it with entertainment systems and a man cave in preparation for the twins.

By the time the twins were resting on their mother's belly, Philip had depleted the remaining startup funds. His father turned him away for a second loan.

After spending a few weeks at home with newborn twins, Philip was raring to try his hand out in the real world again. This time he enlisted his wife's help instead of being beholden to anyone else. He begrudgingly agreed to use money from her trust fund, with a promise to pay back every cent, and the Rosen Foundation was born.

"It's all right," Beau said. "I'll figure it out."

"Call an Uber to pick them up. They'll be fine."

Beau's chest squeezed at the idea, but she didn't want to fight. She really couldn't blame him. Men didn't understand parenting. Not the way a mother did. "Good luck with your meeting, sweetie."

"You too, babe."

Before Beau could say 'I love you,' the line went dead.

She straightened her skirt. She reapplied her lip-gloss and reached into her desk for her emergency mascara. Rolling her neck, she heard the bones crack as the pressure released.

She stood and prepared herself to greet the potential donor. She excelled at this. She was the daughter of a socialite after all.

"Mr. Paulson," Beau reached out her hand to the tall and lanky dark-skinned man who entered her office. "I'm so excited to finally meet you. Thank you so much for making the time to return and speak with me."

She directed him to the guest chair in her office. Though he sat his form in the chair, he was so tall it looked as though he'd only bent over.

"I've been very fortunate in this community," he began. "My mother immigrated here before I was born, and she wasn't the only one. There's a large number of Sudanese refugees living in our community. I want to do something for the children here."

Beau leaned back in her chair. "The Rosen Foundation typically helps children abroad."

"These children began their lives in Sudan. They are the children who escaped the war torn lands. Many have a tough time adjusting to this new way of life; the girls and the boys alike."

Beau took a breath and leaned forward again. "I'm embarrassed to say I've never considered extending our services to the children who make it to our shores."

"I've heard horror stories of organizations raising money and then the money never reaches the needy. Or only a small portion reaches them while the rest is pocketed by the organizations. Not that your organization would ever do that."

"Of course not," Beau said. "We're here to help, and the Rosen Foundation will help the refugees living here in Saint Anne's."

When Beau shook his hand to seal the deal, she noted the time. She had ten minutes to make the twenty-minute trek across town to pick up her kids on time.

Walking Mr. Paulson out, with assurances that she would come up with plans to address the refugee children in the parish, Beau dashed to her car the moment his driver's side door closed. Her car's engine roared to life and she took off across town.

She should feel glad. She'd accomplished so much today. But even through all that hard work, she felt it was her family, her children, who suffered.

She went through her mental rolodex of restaurants that were fast and that the kids liked, because there was no way she was going to have the time and energy to cook dinner tonight. She knew that when she got home there was a mound of laundry to do. Not to mention she had to take a look at the household bills. There was just never enough time in the day.

Speaking of time, she glanced at her dashboard clock. She had three minutes to get to the school before the official end to the Afterschool program. She was five minutes away.

She could do it. She wished she could get there on time for once and not be running late, not be ushering her children in or out of the building like they were in a race. She wished she had time to sleep.

She wished so hard that she missed the red light above her. A bright, white beam of light flashed into her eyes.

Beau caught sight of snow white sheep jumping over a mattress on the side of the truck before she smashed into its side. Her eyes closed and everything went black.

5

The woman before Darrell didn't exactly match her profile. She'd said she was five-nine. She was more like four-nine. Darrell thought maybe that was a typo in the dating app where they'd connected. A woman's height had nothing to do with her kindness.

Janet had mentioned that her body was athletic, but she was more on the curvy side. Which Darrell didn't mind at all. He liked his women with a bit of extra skin. He also liked them thin. He'd never found that the numbers on a scale or a measuring tape made any difference to a woman's intelligence.

Janet had said she was blonde, but her brown roots were showing. That was fine, too. Hair color had nothing to do with a person's loyalty.

Kindness, intelligence, and loyalty; that's all that mattered to Darrell. After a night of filling out survey after poll after questionnaire on the dating app that asked him what he looked for in a woman, he'd narrowed it down to those three items. Sure, he wanted to be attracted to the woman, but looks rated low on the results for his profile.

Getting along with his partner was paramount. Darrell couldn't abide mean-spirited people. His partner would have to have a big heart. He wasn't the most talkative of people, but when he did engage in conversation he also wanted to share his days with someone who would engage his mind. So, intelligence also ranked high on his list. And then there was loyalty. That was the most important thing on Darrell's list.

Even though Janet had fudged a bit on her profile, she was standing up to the first two items on his list. She'd said that she volunteered at a food pantry on weekends as part of her church ministry. And she was smart. She was a programmer at a local tech company. But the best thing about Janet, her eyes hadn't strayed to one of the waiters walking by. A good indication that she might have the loyal trait he was looking for.

"I've had a really good time, Darrell."

And she knew his name to boot. Yes, she was looking like a great candidate.

It was a lunchtime date instead of dinner, like the makers of the dating app suggested for a first date. Darrell and Janet had agreed to meet for a coffee between their busy schedules. He'd had his coffee black. She'd added foam and sugar. There was a study that people who preferred their coffee sweet tended towards kindness.

Janet drained her drink. At the bottom of the cup Darrell saw a lump of crystals gathered at the edge of the Styrofoam. With their drinks finished, they stepped outside of the coffee shop.

"Maybe we could do this again sometime?" Darrell hedged.

Janet looked up at him with a twinkle in her eyes. "I'd like that." She bit her lip and leaned in.

Darrell realized it was his cue for a kiss. He'd never been good at reading those cues, but dating as much as he had over the past few weeks had taught him something.

He leaned down a foot and touched his lips to hers. They were pleasant lips. Thin, but soft. He tasted the sweetness of the sugar at the crease in her lip. He pulled away and she blinked.

"What?" he asked.

"Did you feel it?" she asked.

"Feel what?"

"A spark?"

Darrell frowned.

"You were perfect on paper," Janet sighed. "But no spark."

He blinked again.

"Well..." she sighed. "It was nice meeting you anyway." She turned and trudged down the street.

Darrell stared after her. Could she be serious? They were perfect on paper. And she was going to throw all of that away because there was no static electricity that sparked between their coffee moistened lips?

He threw his hands in the air. He would never understand women.

He made his way back to his office, walking through the market district of the parish. The parish was large enough that he didn't know everyone, but small enough so that faces were familiar. He waved to a few business owners he knew by name or by use of their products.

The walk in the cool air helped to cool him down —a little.

What did women want nowadays? He thought he was approaching modern women who wanted equality. He'd find women with level heads who still had their heads up in the clouds. They spewed gibberish about love at first sight and true love's kiss and golden auras.

It was all nonsense. Just a way to make an excuse for going after someone you lusted after or letting down someone you didn't. Darrell didn't have time for it. He wanted a life partner, a wife. In his case, he would be making that decision based on science and compatibility, not off some imaginary, chemically imbalanced absurdity.

He came up to a building with his name on the glass door. When he'd first begun practicing, he'd shared an office with five other doctors. It had taken him a few years, but now it was solely his name on the office door.

"You have a new patient, Dr. Walker," said his receptionist.

Darrell heard a squeal from the waiting room. He peered in to see two pint-sized human beings. A little girl in a frilly, princess dress, and a boy in scuffed up jeans with a t-shirt that read "Mother's Little Angel." From the looks of them, they were clearly related; twins perhaps?

The little girl stood before the boy with trembling lips as he held something above her head. It was one of the toys Darrell kept in his office to entertain children.

The little boy frowned indignantly at the girl. "I'm going to play with it first. Then maybe you can have a turn."

The little girl didn't argue. Her little shoulders slumped in defeat as though she expected this outcome.

"Hey, buddy," Darrell stepped in. "A gentleman always let's ladies go first."

The little boy looked at Darrell. His wide, blue-gray eyes were the definition of incredulous. "She's not a lady. She's my sister."

"Then it's your job to make sure that all boys, including you, treat her like a lady."

The boy thought on this. He looked at the toy. He looked at his sister.

The little princess' eyes welled with hope. She looked up at Darrell as if she'd never thought anyone would ever take her side. But then the boy turned on his heel and ran into a corner with the toy clutched in his grasp.

Darrell reached up on a shelf and took down another toy. It was a stretch to call the wooden board with colored marbles a toy. The game was the child version of the adult game, Sudoko. In the child version, the player had to arrange the colored marbles in a unique pattern using logic.

"Here," he said to the little girl. "This game is only for the smartest children with the biggest imaginations."

Her eyes widened in the same incredulous shape as her brother's had. Her brother peered from his hiding place.

"Are you smart?" Darrell asked.

She bobbed her dark curls enthusiastically.

"Do you have an imagination?"

"My mommy says I have my head in the clouds. That's where my imaginary friend, Milly, lives."

Darrell looked down into the little girl's light eyes. Like her brother's eyes, there was gray on the outer rims of her irises and blue in the center. It was a startling combination. He wondered where her parents were.

The child took the game from his hands with the greatest care. "Thank you," she said as if he'd just slain a dragon for her.

"Well done, my dear."

Darrell knew that voice. For a moment his lonely heart swelled with joy as Gale Charmayne came into view. Her gray eyes twinkled at him just like the little girl's had. But then he remembered another pair of gray eyes. Kind, intelligent gray eyes that had promised loyalty, and stabbed him in the back as soon as he turned around.

"Ms. Charmayne," Darrell said coolly.

Gale sighed. "Dear heart, you can't begrudge another for finding their truth. Especially not when yours is just around the corner."

Gale had said those words to him a year ago when he found his friend Manny Charmayne kissing his girlfriend in a closet. Manny had insisted that Pumpkin, Darrell's girlfriend, was *The One* he'd been searching for his whole life; his golden girl. Darrell had always listened to the tales of the Charmayne family in good humor, until the fabrications came to bite him in the ass.

Gale had determined that love was on its way to Darrell. But that had been a year ago. His good humor and patience had gone over six months ago.

"Is there something I can help you with, Ms. Charmayne?" Darrell pulled his professionalism around his shoulders like a heavy cloak.

"No," she smiled sadly. "I'm just helping to watch these rascals while their mother sees you. She was in a car accident the other day. I made sure to bring her to the best doctor in the state."

"I appreciate your business." Darrell grabbed the chart and turned away.

He walked down the hall, and slipped into his office. Pulling on his white coat, he gave his hands a wash, and then headed next door into the exam room.

He opened the door quietly. The woman on the exam table had her eyes closed. She lay back with her dark hair fluffed around her heart-shaped face.

Darrell's heart stuttered in his chest. He'd always told himself that beauty wasn't important enough to be on his list. But this woman, lying peacefully on his exam table, made him a liar.

She looked the way every fairytale princess would if they stepped out of a storybook. Her complexion was olive toned. Her eyelashes lay thick on her cheekbones. Her lips were plump and naturally red, with no glossy help. In her repose, her breasts perked up to the sky. He spied long, shapely calves outlined beneath the light fabric of her skirt.

Darrell held still for fear that a step would send him fumbling like a buffoon. He had the urge to go over and kiss her lips to wake her, as in a fairytale. But as soon as he took a step, her eyes opened. He halted immediately as he looked into pale gray eyes.

"Mrs. Charmayne." Darrell's jaw tightened around the surname.

Her brow creased in confusion. "No. My last name is Rosen. Isabeau Rosen."

Darrell blinked. Had he gotten it wrong? Was she not one of Manny's relatives?

"Charmayne was my mother's maiden name," she smiled up at him.

It was the charming Charmayne smile. Darrell looked away and down at his paperwork. His feet unrooted from the spot and he made his way to the small desk beside the exam table. He put the papers down, preparing to sit. Thought better of it, and picked the papers back up. He turned to speak directly to Mrs. Rosen.

That was a mistake.

Isabeau Rosen watched him thoughtfully, expectantly. No interest in her eyes, as there shouldn't have been. He clearly spied the diamond rock on her left hand.

Darrell cleared his throat. "What seems to be the problem, Mrs. Rosen?"

"I was in a car accident the other day."

"I'm sorry to hear that."

"Luckily, it was minor. I was cleared from the hospital with only a few minor bruises, but they recommended seeing a chiropractor to assess if there was any trauma to my spine."

Darrell nodded, slipping fully into professional mode. "That was wise," he agreed. Often times, people in car accidents leave the scene on their own accord only to feel the impact a day or two later when the spine finally registers it.

"My Aunt Gale said you were the best, and my cousin Manny agreed."

Darrell only nodded.

"Do you know my cousin?" she asked.

"We were friends."

"*Were*?"

Darrell ignored the question. "I'll need you to turn over." He indicated the exam table.

She did as she was told and lay on her front.

"I'm going to fold your blouse up a bit so that I can have access to your spine. I apologize if my hands are cold." Darrell reached for the bottom of her shirt. When his fingers made contact with her skin a spark zapped his hand.

He jerked his hand away as she jumped.

"Looks like I've got a bit of static cling there," she smiled apologetically over her shoulder.

Darrell nodded giving his hand a shake. He wiped his hand on his pants and reached for her shirt again. This time there was no spark between them. He placed his hand under her shirt and got down to work.

There was nothing remarkable about her spine. He felt tons of tension in the tendons. "Were you driving while tired, Mrs. Rosen?"

She sighed in answer.

He'd seen it time after time. Women who ran themselves ragged. His mother had been a prime example. He'd had to wrestle her into retirement. Even today, she still insisted on working part time rather than taking his money to relax on.

Darrell knew that when he was married he'd insist that he and his wife share all duties and he'd be more than willing to up his share when he saw that she was overwhelmed. There was no sense in one of them running themselves ragged and then forcing the other one to take over one hundred percent.

No, he knew that the best working relationships were the ones where everyone worked to their strengths. Not exactly an even distribution, but a distribution where they kept an eye out for the other. Mrs. Rosen obviously didn't have that type of arrangement with her husband.

"It's just been busy at work," she said. "And I was rushing to get the kids and—"

"It's okay." Darrell laid a hand at the center of her back and she instantly quieted. He felt some of the tension seep out of her with just that much of a touch. "I'm going to do some adjustments now. The sound may startle you."

Darrell went about contorting Mrs. Rosen's body into the positions to put her spine back into alignment. She didn't jerk from him or tense up. She closed her eyes and allowed him complete control of her body.

Darrell finished his work, giving Mrs. Rosen a light massage to allow the muscles time to resettle. He knew they would come out of alignment in another day or two, so she'd need to schedule a series of appointments until she was healed and the adjustments held.

Darrell grabbed his charts to record his notes. When he

looked up at Mrs. Rosen she hadn't moved. She was resting peacefully. Her eyes closed, her head resting on the exam table. This happened every once in a while with patients. Once the pressure released they were able to find peace and slip into sleep.

Looking closely at her, Darrell saw the dark circles under her eyes. He decided to let her sleep for a few minutes more. Even though he no longer cared for her cousin, it didn't mean he didn't feel for the plight of women who tried to take on the world alone.

Just as there were no fairytale princesses there were no super women. Just every day women who took on too much. Which reminded him, he needed to call his mother today.

He pulled a blanket over Mrs. Rosen. A spark of electricity zapped his fingertips when he lightly brushed her skin. She stirred but did not wake. Darrell shook his fingers and left the room.

6

---

*B*eau floated on a cloud. Her body felt weightless. The last thing she remembered was the sound of snap, crackle, and popping as strong fingers released pressure from somewhere deep inside her. With the release of the pressure came peace.

Her eyes closed and she fell. She wasn't afraid of the fall. It was always how her dreams began. Her fears had come out of the darkness that had plagued her these last five years. The dark cloak of slumber strapped her in like a straightjacket, stifling her Sight.

She hadn't seen anything in her dreams shortly after meeting her own dream man. She'd become pregnant relatively quickly, after a morning of passion where the protection slipped both of their minds. But she hadn't needed her Sight after looking into Philip's eyes. She'd realized the gift had left her when she found out she was pregnant.

Beau had assumed her loss of Sight had something to do with the transition into motherhood. Her sleep cycles had gotten off when she was pregnant. Her body had never grown accustomed to carrying the weight of two additional human beings. After her bundles of joy were brought into the light of the world, the joy of sleep did not return to her. Instead the cloying dark void ruled her nights. But not today.

She wasn't restricted by wispy shadows in this dream. Through the darkness she saw the familiar patches of green, the bright bursts of color. She smelled the heady, floral scents. She felt the bright sun on her skin. Beau's feet landed on the solid earth of her dream garden.

Most of the Charmaynes were gifted with seeing their true love's aura. But Beau and her twin brother, Guy's, Sights differed. Guy was able to see while he was awake. He saw the auras of the talented. He was a hotshot talent agent up in New York.

Beau didn't see anything magical during her waking hours. Her gifts came to life when she lay down to dream. It wasn't an uncommon gift in the Charmayne clan.

Beau's dreams always began and ended in this garden. Her aunt Gale told her that her garden dreams represented a paradise; the world in its ideal form. But Gale had warned Beau that what she saw there wasn't necessarily the future, just a hint at the upcoming possibilities.

Beau had seen her elementary school teacher and the crossing guard. She'd seen the flower shop widow and the piano teacher. Both of those couples were still happily married to this day. And they weren't the only visitors she'd come across in her dream garden.

She'd seen the spinster librarian, Ms. Brown, picking roses one night in her garden. The woman pricked her finger on a thorn. The blood spilled on a green petal and then on the earth. A man loomed over her with white gauze and wrapped the wound.

Beau had rushed to the library the next day, but Ms.

Brown was nowhere to be seen for weeks. The next time she saw Ms. Brown at the library she was getting out of a town car with a cast on her right arm and a ring on her left hand. She'd broken her arm and the young doctor who fixed her up also stole her heart. Beau hadn't dreamed the wound exactly as it happened in reality, but the love between Dr. and Mrs. Ross was very real.

In her present dream, Beau made her way through the garden. She leaned over and smelled the roses. Her every sense came alive in the dream. The sweet, earthy smell of daffodils tickled the hair in her nostrils. Her fingers felt the velvety smoothness of the petals. She heard the crunch of twigs under her feet.

She felt a gentle hand at her back, sliding down her spine. That was new. It wasn't sensual. It relaxed her, allowed her to slip deeper into the dream. She stood and looked over her shoulder, but there was no one there.

In the distance she saw a man standing. Beau's heart sped up. This was the last dream she'd had, the one that had changed her life. She had started having this fantasy-man dream when she went off to college. She was certain she'd find her One on campus. Her heart raced at every man who donned a gray suit, but it had taken four years for Philip to show up.

She smiled at his back now, broad and familiar. She'd spent the last six years resting her head in the crook of that neck. She'd run her hands through that dark, shaggy hair.

Only the hair looked much shorter from this distance. The curls were tight to his head instead of an artful shaggy array. That was odd. Philip hated to have his hair too short. Her dream man had always had long hair, hadn't he?

Well, of course he had, because her dream man was Philip. He was standing there in his gray suit like he'd done when she'd first dreamed him, like he'd been standing the first time she'd seen him six years ago. Though now he looked a bit taller than he had in that dream...

Well, she'd had the dream when she was younger, so of course he had grown a bit. Right? A prickle started up Beau's spine. Her footsteps faltered on the garden's path.

Her dream man began to turn as he always did, signaling the approaching end of the dream. She'd never seen his face in the dream. But she hadn't needed to. She'd known Philip on sight. Especially when she saw him in that tailored suit that fit his trim form to a T. But had her dream man's shoulder's always been that broad?

The prickle up her spine lodged in her throat. Beau felt the urgent need to get to the man in the suit before the dream ended, to see his face in her mind's eye and match it to the reality she saw every day. She tried to hurry her footsteps so that she could reach him, so that she could settle down the prickle.

It was Philip. It had to be Philip. It had always been Philip.

The man began to turn his broad shoulders towards her. There was something off about his jawline. His face seemed longer, where Philip had a perfectly round face.

The prickle turned to bees in her stomach. She felt herself being pulled out of the dream and into wakefulness. She took off running in the dream, trying to get to her dream man. But she couldn't get any closer. He continued to turn but the light around his face dimmed.

Beau jerked into wakefulness.

It wasn't like every morning where she'd barely slept a wink and woke tired. She felt as though she'd slept for months. Her body felt light, alive, energized. It was only her head that was heavy and fogged.

"Feeling better?"

Beau turned to the desk in the corner of the room. Dr. Walker sat, his tall body bent over the desk. His broad shoulders straightened and he turned to her. A pair of glasses on his long, brown face. The hooks rested in his tightly curled hair before disappearing behind his ears. His smile was cool and professional.

"What happened?" she asked. "What time is it?"

"You've been asleep for close to an hour. I sent Gale and your children down to the Fro-Yo shop to let you rest."

Beau frowned at him. She'd been asleep for an hour? But she had so much to do. She swung her legs over the table.

"Whoa, whoa." Dr. Walker was on her, trying to stall her progress. "Your body went through trauma in that car accident. You may feel strong after that adjustment, but you still need to take it easy."

"I can't believe I slept for an hour," she said.

"Your body obviously needed it."

"I haven't slept like that in months, years probably."

"That's not healthy," Dr. Walker tsked. "You need to let your body rest."

"I suffer from insomnia."

He nodded. "How long has this been going on?"

Beau shrugged. "Awhile."

"A few weeks?"

Beau scrunched her nose.

"Months?"

Beau waggled her head, neither in an affirmative yes, nor in a definitive no.

Dr. Walker's eyes widened. "More than a year?"

She felt too embarrassed to confirm it. "I'm the mother

of twins. They came into this world together, but they don't like to go to sleep at the same time."

"Even now that they're older?"

Beau crossed her arms over her chest, her spine going rigid. "I'm a busy woman. I have a business to run, and children to take care of, and a household—"

She stopped as he rose with his hands outstretched to her. Her eyes fixated on his large hands. They'd worked magic on her, sending her into a sound sleep that had allowed her to dream for the first time in years. She wanted that back. She placed her tan hand in his brown one. His hands reminded her of the rich soil in her dream garden. His palm felt strong and warm as he helped her down off the exam table.

"You have to take better care of yourself, Mrs. Rosen."

Beau nodded, eyes still on his hands. "Can you help me?"

He blinked, letting her hand go. Beau willed her fingers not to grip. When she let him go she felt cold disappointment wash over her.

"I've seen a chiropractor before," she said. "But I've never been affected that way. I've never fallen asleep like that. It's like you have magic hands or something."

He frowned. "Not magic. Just years of schooling and practice."

"I was wondering if you could do it again?"

"Do what again?"

"Whatever it is that you did to put me to sleep."

"We can schedule another appointment for two days from now."

"No, no. I need to get back to sleep right now."

Dr. Walker nodded in agreement, but said, "You need to go home and rest."

"I can't. And even if I did manage to put myself to sleep, I don't know if I can get back into the dream on my own."

Dr. Walker took a step back from her.

"Listen, this may sound crazy," she began, and then paused. How was she going to explain to this man, this stranger, that she needed him to do his magic to her spine, to put her back to sleep, so that she could see a man in her dream turn around to confirm that it was indeed her husband of six years? "You know my family? You've heard about... the magic?"

Dr. Walker's frown deepened. "Mrs. Rosen, I'm a man of science. I don't believe in magic."

"Then this definitely will sound crazy to you," she sighed. "You see, I knew I was supposed to marry my husband because I saw him in a dream. But I never actually saw his face. Then I stopped having the dream after I had my children. My sleep cycles went off and never came back on. Until now. Just now I had one of those dreams and..."

Dr. Walker was listening to her rambling with a polite, professional expression that masked disbelief and incredulity. He was probably flipping through his mental Rolodex of psychiatrist colleagues.

"The thing is," she tried again, "because I don't sleep well, I don't dream anymore. You just got me to sleep, and I dreamed. I dreamed for the first time in years, and I want you to do it again."

"It's not magic, Mrs. Rosen. It's science."

"Don't you believe in true love, Dr. Walker?" Was it her imagination or did he recoil?

"I believe in compatibility, partnership, and—" His phone chimed, cutting him off.

Beau glanced over and saw a garish red heart on the face of his phone with the picture of a pretty woman. It was an alert, not a phone call. The header over the heart logo said Gage. Beau recognized the name from all the late night infomercials she watched on television. Gage was the newest dating app that promised to match its users based on fifty points of compatibility. It looked like Dr. Walker had someone interested in engaging with him.

Dr. Walker pocketed the device and headed for the door. "Why don't I leave you to gather your things."

He was out the door before she could make another plea. But she wasn't giving up. Dr. Walker was the first remedy that worked against her insomnia. His magic hands were the first cure to bring back her dreams.

One way or another, she vowed, she'd get those hands on her again. And, now that she knew his dating status, she thought she just might have a way in.

7

Don't you believe in true love?

Darrell couldn't get those gray eyes out of his head. Of course a woman like Isabeau Charmayne Rosen had had men trailing at her feet professing true love. And of course she'd magically found it without any trials.

Don't you believe in true love?

What did that even mean? True love? Love wasn't true or false. It wasn't even quantifiable. The heart was a highway system to funnel blood throughout the body. It had no gage to measure an unquantifiable emotion such as this elusive idea known as love, which couldn't then be quantified as true or false because there was no intrinsic value. The whole equation was null.

Love was an idea, an excuse, a pipe dream. You woke up from dreams. Those dreams would change or fade in the waking hours.

For someone who worked with their hands every day, Darrell trusted what was tactile not chemical. He trusted numbers, data. Data said that over half of marriages ended in divorce. He believed that was because people chose their partners based on an imaginary, unquantifiable, temporary, chemical reaction.

He wished he'd lived during the times of arranged marriages. When unions were determined based on economical and practical matters. There was no practical or economical advantage to love matches, then or now. The first world divorce rate was high, but in places like India and Africa, where they still arranged marriages, divorces were lower.

Darrell had been born in the wrong time. He had viable skills that any family or clan would want. He'd like an old woman to match him up with the perfect candidate where they would suit each other for a lifetime and enrich their community to boot.

He looked out the window and caught sight of Gale and the twins heading back towards the office. Ice cream streamed down the children's cheeks. Darrell turned away from Gale and looked at his cell phone. He may not have a matchmaker, but he did have today's equivalent.

Another alert sounded on his phone. Another match through the Gage app. He took a second to look through the woman's profile, wanting to avoid another mismatch like his coffee date from earlier. The app guaranteed that it would match potential couples on fifty levels of compatibility, but he knew no system was foolproof.

Darrell took a look at those levels from his newest match and frowned. Where he had an advanced degree, this woman had a GED. Where his hobbies included chess, hers was slam poetry. She was twenty-two, he was thirty-two. His eyes tightened on the screen. They were not compatible. Why was he constantly getting alerts from women who weren't his ideal?

Darrell switched over to look at his profile. He had three

pictures, like the website suggested. A profile shot of him in his office, dressed in his white doctor's coat. A long shot of him outside his office building, which had been taken when he opened his practice. His name read prominently on the face of the building. And then a fun shot of him at the community center, teaching chess.

These images showed his personality. He was dedicated, serious; a hard worker who gave back to his community.

An inbox message alert popped up in his profile. It was from this new mismatch. She wanted to get together for dinner. She suggested going out to one of the most exclusive restaurants in the city. Darrell deleted the message.

Another match alert popped up. This new match was age-appropriate. She had a number of letters behind her name to indicate her professionalism. But one glance at her profile told him that she was looking for a true connection with 'the one.' Bile rose in Darrell's throat at the sight of those two words.

He shut his phone off and shoved it into his pocket. He glared at the closed door of the exam room. Mrs. Rosen hadn't emerged yet.

Don't you believe in true love?

No, he did not believe in true love. He didn't play around with such childish, fanciful things for such an important a decision as to whom he would spend the rest of his life with, make a family with.

"Are you all finished then?"

Darrell turned around to the smiling face of Gale Charmayne. "Yes," he said. "She'll be out in a minute."

"Is my mommy gonna be okay?"

Darrell bent down to be on level with the little girl who had her mother's face and startling, light eyes. "She's going to be fine. She just needs to rest. You'll have to be a big help to her for a few days. Maybe help by keeping your room clean, and helping out at dinner."

The little girl nodded, but another voice pipped in.

"But mommy cleans our room and makes dinner."

Darrell, still down on his haunches, swiveled around to face the little man. "Well, mommy needs to rest so she can get her strength back. You can help your dad out with the cooking."

"Daddies don't cook," the little man insisted.

Darrell's eyebrows rose up to his hairline. He nodded his head in that way when you disagreed with a statement, but searched your brain for a tactful way to respond.

"Our dad works a lot," supplied the little girl as she leaned against Darrell. Her small body burrowed into him like a kitten seeking a head scratch.

"Yeah," agreed her brother. "He plays a lot of golf. The game where you hit the ball with the stick. But the ball is little and it's on the ground. Not like baseball when you have to hit the ball while it's still in the air."

Darrell looked at Gale who watched the kids with amusement. "They're father's a professional golf player?" he asked.

Gale suppressed a grin and appeared to consider her answer.

"No, he's not," insisted the little girl. "He works in a building with mommy and he helps sad people."

"Sad people?" Darrell asked.

The little girl nodded. "People without any money or houses or food."

"Their parents run the Rosen Foundation," supplied Gale.

Darrell had heard of the Rosen Foundation. The community center he volunteered for had mentioned the organization before, as a potential source of donations, but they'd been denied the monies because they were a local organization and the Rosen Foundation only gave to international matters.

"My daddy is my mommy's boss," said the boy. "Men and bosses don't cook. They also don't have to keep their rooms clean."

The little girl shook her head vehemently. "Nun unh, mommy's the boss."

The little boy crossed his arms over his little chest, preparing for what looked like another tantrum.

Darrell had heard enough. He stood just as Isabeau Rosen came out of the exam room and down the hall. The little girl rushed to her mother's side.

"Flora, honey," Mrs. Rosen admonished. "What did mommy say about running?"

The little girl skid to a halt. Her shoulders slumped. Her mother patted her on the head and continued on to her brother.

"Did you enjoy your ice cream, Faun?" Mrs. Rosen rubbed at his stained cheek. Faun ducked away from his mother's touch.

Flora and Faun? Darrell hoped those were nicknames. What self-respecting man would agree to his son being named after a deer? But it was none of his business.

Mrs. Rosen straightened and wobbled on her ascent. Darrell reached out to her, placing his hand at the small of her back to offer support. She needed to get home and rest. For the first time in a year, he had the urge to call Manny and enlist his help. Surely, Manny could get his cousin to take it easy. But that was a number he was unlikely to dial ever again.

When Darrell went to remove his hand, Mrs. Rosen

grabbed his fingers and locked them within her grip. Her gray eyes were wide with a plea.

"This might sound crazy," she said. "But I think you were in my dream."

"You're dreaming again, my dear?" asked Gale.

Mrs. Rosen nodded at her aunt with a brilliant smile on her face. "I was back in my dream garden. I had the dream again, the one about Philip."

Gale's lips pinched together, as though she were considering the response. But her niece didn't seem to notice.

"He was about to turn around," Mrs. Rosen continued, her fingers still locked in a death grip around Darrell's. "I was so close to seeing him. But it was different this time. I felt another presence. I think it was Dr. Walker."

Both women turned to gaze at him.

"What could that mean?" Mrs. Rosen asked.

"Maybe you two are on the same karass?" Gale offered.

Darrell rolled his eyes. He'd heard Gale say the same thing about his ex-friend, Manny, and his ex-girlfriend, Pumpkin. He wasn't on any karass. Darrell had been left firmly ashore while those two had sailed off into the sunset.

"In the past, I was known as something of a matchmaker," Mrs. Rosen said. "I've seen a number of couples together in my dream. And, the next thing you know, they got married. All of them are still together to this day."

Darrell had heard a few of the tales of the Charmayne clan. He knew Gale saw auras and claimed to be psychic. He knew Manny had a male cousin who saw something or other about golden talent. He'd even heard about another cousin who had some type of magic, healing touch. He couldn't remember if he'd heard about this particular cousin who saw love matches in her dreams, but he didn't care. It was a fool's idea to entrust such a huge decision to someone's imagination while they slept.

"You don't have to believe me," Mrs. Rosen said. "But will you at least help me?

"Help you how?" Darrell tried again to disentangle his fingers from hers. She reluctantly let them go.

"I want to come in for another adjustment tomorrow," she said.

Darrell hesitated. He didn't want to encourage this wild behavior.

"Please?" She pulled her lip into her mouth; much like her daughter had done when her brother wouldn't let her play with his toy.

Darrell was also a sucker for a quivering lip. "You can come back in two days."

Mrs. Rosen's face fell. But it couldn't be helped.

"You have to allow your body time to receive the adjustment," he said. "Besides, it's Friday and I'm not open on the weekends."

She nodded her head in defeat.

"Over the weekend I need you to take it easy," he continued. "You have to rest."

"I will," she agreed readily.

"You can't drive."

"My insurance company declared my car totaled."

"You'll need to stay at home and take the day off on Monday as well."

She grimaced. "That's going to be difficult. I have to drive the kids to school in the morning, and then there's work..."

"Your husband can take the children."

Her eyebrows went into her hairline as though the idea

was so preposterous that it sailed over her head. "He's not very good with kids."

"They're his kids." Then again, with all the modern women he'd been dating lately, maybe he shouldn't make that assumption. "Aren't they?"

"Yes." Indignation coated her voice.

Darrell held up his hands. Another thing he didn't understand about modern women was that if they believed in equal pay, then they should believe in equal distribution of all work, including the household duties. She'd had trauma to her person and she would need her partner to lend a hand or two. But it wasn't his place to get into her marriage.

He got her to agree to a few more aftercare regimens, and then he ushered the bunch of them out the door, with little Flora trailing behind. The little girl gave his leg a squeeze before catching up with the rest of her family.

Darrell felt sorry for the poor thing. She was clearly trapped in a family that didn't give her enough attention. She also had a grown mother who believed in fairytales. That clearly affected the little girl if she looked up at Darrell as a possible knight in shining armor when he wore a white coat. The only knights he acknowledged were those that were on the chessboard.

8

———

*B*eau didn't realize she'd shut her eyes until she found herself falling through the dream. At first, her conscious mind jerked and resisted. But instead of the darkness confining her, like it had done the last six years, she floated down through a sunlit sky and landed on her feet. The plush ground came to greet her bare toes. The roses in the bushes opened their blooms in salutation. Beau ran her fingers over the blooms, certain to steer clear of the thorns.

In the distance she saw her dream man. No, not her dream man. Her husband. Philip. It was Philip.

Please, god, let it be Philip.

She crept nearer to him. Slowly. Afraid any sudden movements might wake her from the dream before he turned around.

He stood in his gray suit, looking out into the distance. As Beau came up closer, she stared at his broad shoulders. Philip was lean. He had been leaner when they first met. His body hadn't changed that much in years. He hadn't put on any weight at all since he always made time to get to the gym.

Beau had softened around the middle after having children and sitting behind a desk most days. Her gym membership went untouched since she had the children to take care of in the afternoon, and dinner to put on the table in the evening, which often turned out to be fatty restaurant foods instead of home cooked meals.

But still, even though Philip kept fit, he was not that broad. He also was not that tall. And then there was the hair. It was the wrong texture. But he was hazy through the dream. Beau squinted to get a better look.

Her dream man stood in the sun, but his body was cast in a shadow. She tried to pick her feet up to move closer. But she felt her body moving slowly.

A hand came to rest at her back. It was warm and steady. It anchored her, but not in a confining way. It steadied her; its weight making her feel lighter. She turned to look over her shoulder, expecting to see nothing behind her. But there was something behind her. There was someone.

This had never happened before in this dream. When she'd seen couples in the past, they had been in another part of her dream garden. It had always been only Philip and her in this particular part of the garden; the part that overlooked the cliff. She'd land in this spot and see him. He'd start to turn and she'd wake up.

Beau blinked in the dream. The shape behind her broke free from the haze of her mind. A tall figure with an angular face came into focus. Was that...?

Yes, it was Darrell Walker. Dr. Walker had his hand at her back. He smiled down at her. She'd thought his eyes were dark brown, but they weren't. There were flecks of hazel in them. Like sand mixed with soil. His smile was gentle, reassuring. It wasn't the professional smile he gave his patients. This had to be the smile he gave his friends.

A spot in her heart warmed for him. Her aunt would call the warming a premonition. Beau knew then that she and Darrell would be great friends.

Someday.

Once he learned to believe in magic. That would be her first task as his friend; to teach him that there was magic in the world. To make him see that the magic all began with love.

With that decision made, Beau relaxed into her new friend's hand. But the moment she settled, Darrell pulled the hand away.

On his wrist she caught sight of a gold watch. The time-piece looked ancient and expensive with brownish stones in the face. The hands of the watch had stopped.

Darrell turned from her, pointing his finger at some-thing off in the distance. His fingers crooked, beckoning the hazy shape forward. Beau couldn't make it out. She didn't really care to know what the other shape was. There was another shape she had to decipher.

She turned around, away from the unknown shape, away from her new friend, and back to the man of her dreams. In her heart, she knew it was Philip. But when she turned back to the cliff, her dream man was gone.

The sound of birds called Beau to open her eyes. She woke to the sun planting soft kisses on her cheek. A bird chirped a sweet song on the branch outside her bedroom window. The bed was warm and the room was bright.

It had been years since she'd slept through the night. She felt giddy. She stretched her limbs over her head and then out to the sides, only to find that the bed was empty.

There was a note from Philip on the dresser. It read: Decided to let you sleep in. Gone to the gym. ~P

Beau's heart warmed at the thoughtfulness of her dream man. He didn't need to turn around inside her mind to show her that he was everything she'd ever hoped for in a partner.

The house was quiet in the early morning light. Gale had agreed to watch the kids overnight, to give Beau a break. Last night, Faun had frowned and whined when his mother left Gale's car and he remained strapped in. Poor Faunie didn't like any deviation from his routine. Flora, thankfully, sat quietly in her seat.

Beau worried that Gale would tire of the children and their little tantrums. She was sure to tell her aunt that the best way to calm Faun down was to give him a hug to make him feel secure. Her aunt nodded and pulled out of the driveway as Faun continued to whine in the backseat of the car.

Beau had assumed all went well since Gale hadn't returned them in the middle of the night or called her this morning for an early pickup. It wasn't like it was her aunt's first time with rowdy twins. She'd watched Beau and Guy when they were that age.

Beau had fallen asleep shortly after they pulled off. She had vague memories of Philip climbing into bed beside her late last night. She wished he'd stayed with her until she woke up so that they could've had some time alone together. She couldn't remember the last time they'd stayed in bed for a day, or an evening, or a morning.

Beau took her time rising. There was stiffness in her spine and minor aches in her bones. She ignored the twinges of discomfort. She felt refreshed, reborn.

She opened the curtains to the bright sun and chirping

bird. After a leisurely shower, she dressed in a sundress and headed down the hall. She poked her head into Flora's room. She smiled as she noted that everything was in order in her daughter's room. Faun's room was a different story and Beau took thirty minutes to straighten his toys, clothes, and bed.

After that, she spent the morning trying to take it easy. And by trying to take it easy, she logged into her email and the office's shared drive. She had promised Dr. Walker that she wouldn't go into the office, and she wasn't in the office physically. A worker didn't have to go into the office these days, with smart phones and the Cloud. The office was open 24/7.

Add to that the fact that Beau was a working mother and motherhood was also a 24/7 job, and it was a wonder she got any sleep at all. But she had gotten her fair share of sleep last night. And now that she was awake again, her brain couldn't turn off.

Why did the man in her dreams suddenly have a different physicality than her husband? Why had Philip disappeared in her dream? He'd never done that before. And what was Dr. Walker doing in her dream? And what or who was he pointing to off in the distance? Maybe that was the person Darrell Walker was supposed to be with, his true love?

She went outside to get some fresh air. She had a small garden in her back yard. The weeds had overtaken much of the small patch, due to her negligence. Beau got down on her knees and dug into the soil.

The cool earth felt good in her hands. It settled her overworked mind. With her attention turned from work, she focused on her home life.

Dr. Walker did have a point. She couldn't let the dream

get to her like that. She and Philip had a great marriage. They complemented each other in so many ways. She was organized and methodical to his impulsive, risk-taking habits. She was a social butterfly to his caterpillar-in-a-corner nature. And there were many other ways they complemented each other, ways that she couldn't think of right at this moment.

She arched her back and felt a twinge. She took her time getting to her feet from her kneeling position in the garden. Perhaps she had overdone it? But it had been such a long time since she'd had this much time to herself.

A honk from the front of the house drew her around. She went to the front to see Philip arrive in a car not his own. And he wasn't alone. The children were in the back seat. That surprised Beau most of all.

Philip had never taken the kids out on his own. She could only assume this was Gale's doing. Her family often frowned at Philip's lack of involvement with the children. But Beau understood Philip's hesitancy at managing the children. Unlike Beau, who'd grown up in an extended family of younger and older cousins, Philip was an only child born to older parents. He'd always been awkward around any children, including his own.

Philip had been nervous about the idea of having one child. When he learned they were having twins he'd turned green. He was always nervous to hold them, afraid he would drop them, having never held a baby before. He insisted he'd get more involved when they could crawl. By the time the twins were rug-rats, he insisted he'd be able to engage more with them when they walked. Then he wanted to wait until they talked because he didn't understand their gibberish like she did.

Beau's heart warmed to see her family together with her

husband at the helm of the wheel. As he put the car in park, the kids spilled out of the back seat. Faun opened the door and hopped out. Flora tipped over in her car seat. She was strapped into the seat, but the seat wasn't strapped to the car with the seat belt. Beau's heart stopped at the sight.

"Philip you have to strap the seats in."

Philip frowned looking over his shoulder. "They survived."

Beau took a deep breath and opened her arms to Faun. "How was your time with Auntie Gale, Faunie?"

Faun shrugged, rounding his mother and heading into the house. Flora, having freed herself from the car seat, hopped out of the car with a piece of paper in hand.

"Do you want to see what I drew at Auntie Gale's, mommy?"

"In a minute, Flora." Beau's attention was on the new car. The car had a bow on top of the hood.

Philip walked towards her with keys in hand. "Surprise."

"What's this?" Beau asked.

"What's it look like?" He came over and pecked her on the cheek.

"It looks like a new car."

"It's your new car, since your old one was declared a total loss."

"We can't afford a new car," she said. That wasn't exactly true. She could afford a new car with the money in her trust, but they had agreed to live off their salaries from the foundation.

"It's a company car," he said.

"The company can't afford a car, Philip." Especially not an expensive, luxury car.

"I signed the consultant, Yohance Stanley. It was his idea. We can write it off on our business taxes and save a huge amount of money for ourselves. He's already figured out a ton of other ways that we can make more money. And with the new car, you can take the kids to and from school on Monday."

"The doctor told me not to get back behind the wheel yet."

"What doctor? The chiropractor? That's not a real doctor. You're fine. Besides, I can't chauffeur the kids around all day. I have meetings to get to."

He pulled dry cleaning from the back. None of the suits looked anything like the suits she'd previously washed and hung up in his closet a few days ago.

"Those are new?" she asked.

He nodded.

"They're dark blue."

"Yeah, you always get me gray suits. You know how much I hate gray."

"You love gray," she said. "It's your favorite color."

"No," Philip shook his head. "It's your favorite color. I keep telling you that but you never listen to me."

He rounded her and went into the house.

Beau looked down at Flora who still waited patiently to show her mother her drawing. Beau smiled at her daughter and took the picture. It was of a man on a horse with a sword. He had a brown Crayola face and a white doctor's coat.

9

"Thank you, Dr. Walker. I had an enjoyable time."

"Thank you, Dr. Paley. I'll have to be sure and look up your paper on the effectiveness of epidural injections for disc herniation."

"I think you'll find it riveting. Be sure and look out for the joke about lumbars." She chuckle-snorted.

It was a loud snort and a few people on the sidewalk jerked their heads up from their handheld devices.

When Darrell turned back, Dr. Paley had her hand extended. He should've felt relief that the pressure to interpret the farewell was taken out of his hands. He took her capable hand in his. Her handshake was firm.

"I feel that we have a good deal of potential," she said.

"Potential?"

"As partners. We have a lot of the same interests, a similar temperament, and career goals that are in alignment. We make perfect sense."

They did. Darrell couldn't find a reason to disagree to their union. Or at least a second date.

He looked down at her hand, which still gripped his. He

looked up into her face. He didn't need any paper to help him interpret the look on her face. It was one of assessment, not a hint of passion. But did one require passion in a relationship?

Before his mind could wrap around the mental query, something bowled into his thighs. He looked down to see a thick mop of hair surrounding a cherubic face with bright blue-gray eyes. Flora Rosen was wrapped around his leg.

Dr. Paley jumped back with a yelp as though she saw a mouse scamper across her penny loafers.

Flora looked up at Darrell with a gap-toothed grin. He couldn't help smiling back down at the little angel. He was often awkward with adults and people his own age. But kids he understood.

"Don't encourage the little thing," said his date. "It might be a part of some street scam."

"Hi, Dr. Walker," giggled Flora.

"Hello, Princess Flora." Darrell may not have believed in fairytales for grown women, but he had no problem pretending with little girls.

"You know this... person?"

Darrell looked up at Dr. Paley. She still eyed the child as though she were a rodent. Well, there was one major level of compatibility where they didn't unite. Darrell tried to think back to if Dr. Paley had indicated her distaste for children on her Gage profile. He was certain he had written down his love and desire for them on his.

"She belongs to one of my patients." Darrell looked around for the girl's mother. He half hoped he didn't find her. Beau Rosen should still be resting.

"Are they allowed to just run around like that?" asked Dr. Paley. The woman had put a few feet of distance between herself and Flora. "Should we call a school or the police or something?"

"Flora, I told you not to walk away from me." Beau Rosen came running up to him. She reached down to disentangle her daughter from Darrell's person. "I'm so sorry, Dr. Walker. She's just super friendly, and she took to you the other day. She drew a picture of you on a horse. I'm afraid you have an admirer."

Darrell had seen this before. The child was starved for attention, particularly male attention. He peered around Beau Rosen and didn't see a man in her shadow. Where was her husband? He saw a key chain swinging on her index finger and a heavy bag slung over her shoulder.

Dr. Paley eyed Beau with the same distaste that she'd eyed her daughter. "You're the child's mother?" she asked tightly, her voice laced with disapproval.

"Yes," Mrs. Rosen said, without missing a beat. "I'm Beau. That's my daughter Flora." She stuck out her hand to Dr. Paley. "And you are?"

Dr. Paley smiled tightly at Beau's offer. "I'm leaving." She turned back to Darrell. "Perhaps we can meet in a more adult arena next time. There's a lecture at the college on spinal health that I'm looking forward to. I look forward to your call, Dr. Walker." Then she turned on her loafered heel and left.

"She's all kinds of wrong for you," Mrs. Rosen said.

Darrell followed her trajectory. Her gray eyes watched Dr. Paley as she crossed the street.

"You need someone lively. Someone to help bring you out of your shell. You're both so closed off." She motioned in the vicinity of his chest.

Darrell knew she might be right. If Dr. Paley disliked children it wouldn't work, because he wanted some of his own. But the last thing he wanted to do was to give a Charmayne the satisfaction of interfering with his life again.

"Do you claim some psychic abilities, too?" he asked.

"I don't need psychic abilities," she said. "I have eyes."

"You don't even know me."

She opened her mouth to argue that point. Darrell wasn't sure how she could. They'd only just met. What could possibly make her think she knew him? Or think that she knew what kind of woman would be good for him?

"Dr. Paley and I are in similar fields," he said. "We have the same amount of education, the same values, the same goals in life."

"Having things in common is important, but opposites often attract. That's science," she smiled.

Darrell shook his head. "Then by your definition, attraction is an electrical phenomenon that only works when one object, or person, is negative, or right side up, and the other is positive, or upside down?"

Mrs. Rosen's brow furrowed. Her daughter looked at him with wide adoring eyes. The unfortunately named little boy stood behind his mother and kicked at a flower peeking its way out of the cement in the sidewalk.

"I'm most interested that you think that positivity is upside down," Mrs. Rosen smiled.

She kept aiming those smiles at him, as though she were trying to be his friend. Darrell didn't need any new friends. He was still recovering from the betrayal of the last one.

"I believe in being methodical about my search for a life partner," he said. "I have no interest in leaving it up to lust or fate or magnetic fields."

"Now I'm fascinated that you put lust in the same category as fate."

"You can make the claim that neither are within your

control," said Darrell. "Science and the scientific method involve a process in a controlled environment with specific steps to test a theory or solve a problem. It seems to me the most appropriate way to go about the search for a partner."

"You can't control who you fall in love with, Dr. Walker. You're friends with Manny and Pumpkin?"

Darrell tensed at the mention of those two names. Even joined together by a conjunction it annoyed him.

"How do you explain the two of them?" Mrs. Rosen asked.

Darrell shook his head instead of responding. He heard his molars grinding.

"Mommy, you said we were going to the park," whined the little boy.

"Sweetie, I know, but the park is under construction right now."

"But I wanna go down the slide."

Mrs. Rosen reached behind her neck and squeezed the space between her shoulder blades. As she did so the bag slipped from her opposite shoulder.

Darrell caught the bag before it hit the ground. It nearly brought him down. The thing weighed a ton. "I thought we agreed that you would take it easy."

"Motherhood is twenty-four-seven." She reached for the bag, but he didn't give it back.

"How are you sleeping?"

She waggled her head. "I slept very well Friday night after your adjustment. But last night..." she shrugged.

"Last night what?" he prompted.

"I did have a really good nap earlier in the day."

A nap was not good enough for healing. "Why don't you come into the Community Center. Let me take a look at that," he pointed to her hands indicating the space where she squeezed at her neck.

Her eyes lit up. The gray parted like clouds to reveal something clear and bright beneath. Isabeau Rosen had one of those smiles that endeared people to her.

Darrell steeled himself. He did not need any more Charmaynes or magic or fairytale characters in his life. She was a client in his care. He would do his due diligence for her and then send her on her way.

"But I wanna go to the park." The little man stomped his foot.

His mother turned to answer him, but Darrell stepped in.

"There're two sliding boards in the rec center. One for little kids that goes straight down. And one for big kids that's long and curvy. I think I can get you onto the big kid slide, but you're going to have to prove to me that you are a big boy."

Intelligent, blue-gray eyes stared back at him with doubt. In the end, childhood curiosity won out. "I am a big boy. My mommy said so."

Darrell looked at Beau, who had a crooked smile on her face as she watched the two of them. "Well, your mother hasn't been to the rec center. So, they'll have to take my word for it. Show me this big boy behavior on our way there and I'll put in a good word for you."

The little man thought this over for all of two seconds before nodding. He puffed his chest out and fell in line as they walked down the street to the center.

Flora maneuvered her tiny hand into Darrell's large one. She took her mother's hand in the other and swung their arms as she skipped in between the adults. It was a short and quiet walk.

"I'm sorry if we're taking you out of your way," Mrs. Rosen said.

Darrell shook his head. "I was heading there anyway. I run the youth chess program."

"Do you work with Pumpkin's son, Seth? He's beaten me every time we've played."

Darrell nodded. "He's on the team. He'll probably be there today."

Walking through the doors of the Community Center, they immediately spied Seth at one of the tables, with a board and pieces before him. It took Darrell one glance to realize his young protégé was losing.

"What's wrong with him?" Darrell asked his father, Anthony.

Anthony had been coming to pick Seth up a lot from the community center since his mother's marriage to Manny. Though Darrell and Pumpkin had cleared the air, it was still awkward when they came face-to-face.

At first Darrell had been standoffish with Anthony. After all, his own father had abandoned him and his mother, leaving them in a tight spot. Anthony had abandoned Pumpkin and Seth, but he'd come back into their lives. From what Darrell could see, it looked like he was making up time with his son.

Anthony sighed as he leaned in to whisper conspiratorially to Darrell. "He's having girl troubles. You remember Kimmei? The little girl who won the talent competition when she sang last year?"

"Yeah." Darrell remembered the little girl and her mother. He'd wanted to ask Midori Miller out on a date, but she was a workaholic like him.

"She got a recording contract and is in New York now. Seth's broken up about it."

Darrell could relate. He patted Anthony on the back and turned back to Mrs. Rosen. "Let the kids go to the rec room."

She twisted her lip. It looked like she was also one of those helicopter parents who didn't let her kids out of her sight. No wonder she was having trouble sleeping and resting.

"They'll be fine," he said.

The kids took off into the indoor playroom. Darrell waited patiently while their mother looked around the room, trying to spy any hidden dangers or suspicious characters. Then finally she followed him into an empty office.

He pulled up a straight-back chair and had her take a seat backwards. He placed his hand on her spine and she let out an audible sigh.

He almost rolled his eyes. What he did wasn't magic. It was science. But it was nice when someone appreciated his work.

"I saw something in my dream," she offered up as he pressed on her low back.

"Hmmm?"

"You were there."

"You do realize that dreams are simply a mental phenomenon occurring during sleep in which images, thoughts, and even emotions are experienced with a sense of reality."

She chuckled. "I've never met someone who resisted magic the way that you do. Well, no. That's not true. My husband didn't believe in my visions either."

"The husband you married after seeing him in a dream?" Darrell wondered how that bit of magic was working out? "Dreams can be a manifestation of our wants.

You likely dreamed of me because you'd met me and you wanted me to help you."

"Well, if so, it worked. Now you're helping me."

Darrell's hands paused.

She chuckled again. "You were helping me, in the dream," she said. "But then I got the feeling I was supposed to help you."

"Help me?" He set to work on her spine again. "How?"

"In the dream, you had your hand on my spine. But then I was standing by you as something was coming towards you. I got the impression that it was a woman. In the past, whenever I dreamed of two people together, they wound up getting married."

His hand jerked away from her spine. "That's…"

"Crazy? In the dream, you had a watch on your wrist. It was a gold watch with brownish stones in the face. But the hands had stopped."

Darrell froze.

She looked over her shoulder at him. "You're not wearing it. But you know what I'm talking about. Don't you?"

"How could you possibly know that?" There were only two other people who knew about that watch. It sat in a box in his attic.

"You might not believe in magic, Dr. Walker. But it seems to me it's constantly surrounding you. My cousin, my aunt, and now me. You are looking for love, aren't you?"

"No," Darrell jerked out of his mind and back to the present. "I'm looking for a life-partner."

"You make marriage sound like a business."

Darrell sighed, instead of arguing with the woman. He ran his hands down her spine and massaged out a kink he found there.

"Why are you so resistant to love?" she said.

"Why are you doubting that you chose the right man to marry?" he countered.

She jerked from his touch. "Philip and I have our ups and downs, like any marriage."

"So, why don't you trust in your love and your magic? Why do you have to check your vision again?"

She let out a shuddery breath. "All of the other couples, I saw each of them clearly. I never saw my husband's face, only his back. I just want to see his face."

"And you think if you can go back to sleep and dream you'll see his face?"

"Yes, but not only his face. I could see your dream girl's face, too. We'd both win. We'd both get exactly what we want."

"I assume the woman you saw wasn't Dr. Paley?"

She sighed; the look on her face was grave. "I'm sorry, but the woman I saw in my dream wasn't wearing penny loafers." She held the grave look for two more seconds before breaking into a grin.

Darrell fought the edges of his mouth from grinning back. Did he want this? To believe in this? He twirled his finger in the air, indicating that she should turn back around. She rolled her eyes and did as she was told. Darrell placed his hands on her spine and worked out the rest of the kinks.

10

"Thank you for doing this, Pumpkin," Beau said, as they idled down the road in Pumpkin's orange Beetle.

Beau knew that her cousin, Manny, had tried to get his wife to replace the Volkswagen with a model from this century. His wife had flat out refused to be parted with the car. So they'd compromised. The Beetle got a complete internal make over, which Beau was sure cost more than the car was originally worth. Today, the Bug buzzed down the street, zipping past the large, growling muscle cars preferred in the parish.

"Don't mention it," Pumpkin smiled from the driver's seat. "It's just nice to hear someone say 'thank you' in this car. My cousins used to expect me to cart them around town like I was their own personal taxi service."

Beau knew that before Pumpkin married Manny she'd had a hard time with her family members. Her parents died when she was young and the family she had left hadn't been welcoming.

Beau could never understand why. She'd liked Pumpkin

the moment she'd met the woman a year ago, shortly after Manny had proposed to her. When Beau was a girl, she'd had a dream of Manny in a field of pumpkins. It all made sense now.

She'd had a dream of her brother in a field of music notes and gold ribbons. She was still hoping that vision would pan out some day. That is, if her brother ever decided to settle down.

Beau knew her twin, Guy, wanted to get married and have a family of his own. He'd even been dating the same girl for over a year now, but something seemed off about the relationship between Guy and his artist, Agave.

Beau had only met the woman once or twice when she'd gone to visit her brother in New York. He didn't encourage any relationship between Agave and his sister, despite Beau's meddling. She doubted Agave was Guy's One. For some reason, she knew that relationship wouldn't turn into a marriage.

"Well, I do thank you," she said to Pumpkin. "Especially for taking my kids off my hands while I visit the good doctor."

Beau looked over her shoulder at her children dozing in the back. They'd had a midday nap yesterday after playing in the Community Center. She should've known better than to have let them sleep in the middle of the day, but the peace and quiet had been too good to pass up. She'd paid for it that night when Faun wouldn't settle down for bed and woke up twice in the middle of the night, crying at her door.

Philip had rolled over, grumbling. It was left up to Beau to settle the child down. After Beau walked Faun back to his room the second time, she'd noticed that Flora was also wide awake. But the child soothed herself, arranging her dolls at the edge of her bed. Flora smiled when she spied her mother in the door.

Beau paused at Flora's door, but Faun whined and pulled her attention away again. She followed him into his room, read him two bedtime stories, rubbed his back, and then rocked him until finally he went to sleep. By then she was left wide awake.

Just as it was difficult getting the boy to sleep at night, it was even worse getting him up in the morning. And now he was dozing in the backseat of the car. But Beau couldn't bring herself to wake either child up while she had a chat with her friend.

"Dr. Walker said I shouldn't drive. He made it a condition of seeing me today."

Pumpkin nodded, but Beau felt the atmosphere change. She knew there was a history with Darrell and Manny. She'd never met Darrell before, despite the fact that she and Manny were close. And why would she have? There hadn't been many occasions for Beau's family and Manny's bachelor friends to hang out. Still, she wondered if there was something she didn't know about the good doctor?

"He and Manny are friends, right?" Beau asked.

"They were friends," Pumpkin said. "Good friends."

"What happened?"

Pumpkin sighed. "We used to date. Darrell and I."

Oh. "Before you and Manny?"

"Well..."

Oh. Now things became a little clearer. It seems Manny had usurped his friend's girl. Or had Pumpkin usurped her boyfriend's friend?

"Darrell's a great guy," said Pumpkin. "He's kind and smart. He's great with Seth. He's a complete gentleman. The kind of man any girl would want."

"But not you?"

Pumpkin shook her head.

"Let me guess? No spark?"

Pumpkin nodded.

Beau and Philip hadn't had that problem. They'd sparked off the Richter scale when they met. It was just lately that there seemed to be a dulling of the senses, a sense that they were out of sync.

"And you and Manny, of course, sparked."

Pumpkin's eyes shone bright. Beau missed that bright glow of being a newlywed. She and Philip hadn't been able to keep their hands off one another from the moment they'd met. That was one reason why they'd gotten pregnant so quickly; before their marriage. Once the kids were born, it was as though the spark had been doused by a double dose of cold water.

They hadn't even been on a date since the twins had been born. Sure they'd gone out to events and dinners and galas, but those were all work related. Everything always related back to work.

"I wish Darrell would find someone special," said Pumpkin. "He deserves it. He does so much work at the community center in his spare time. He gives so much back to the community. He gives so much of himself. If anyone deserves a happy ending it's definitely him."

A happy ending. That's what Pumpkin had with Manny. That's what Beau had with Philip. She rested her head against the headrest and winced. She felt the tension down her entire spine from lack of sleep.

"I just hope he doesn't settle for less than what he's worth," Pumpkin continued. "I also hope that one day he can forgive Manny. Manny misses his friendship."

Pumpkin pulled up outside of Dr. Walker's office. The

good doctor strolled up the sidewalk with a foam cup in his hands. When he spotted the orange Beetle he froze like a deer in headlights.

"Hey, Darrell." Pumpkin called from the rolled down window.

Dr. Walker nodded. "Mrs. Charmayne."

Beside her, Beau heard Pumpkin sigh. She turned to Beau. "I'm going to take the kids to the park across the street."

"Thanks, Pumpkin," Beau said, reaching for the door handle. Before she could, Dr. Walker had it opened for her and offered her his hand.

Beau was startled. It had been a long time since she'd received such gentlemanly services. She took his hand. The static cling that had plagued them the first time they met struck again.

"Sorry," she said.

He looked past her, shutting the car door and offering another stiff smile to Pumpkin. He turned to his office as Pumpkin pulled away from the curb.

Beau fell in step beside him. "Pumpkin was telling me how good of friends you and Manny were. You think you two could ever—"

He pulled the glass door of his office building open and motioned for her to precede him, shutting down the conversation. With that door shut, Beau decided to try another tactic. If he wasn't going to rekindle his friendship with Manny, she decided to double her efforts in sparking a friendship between the two of them.

"I wanted to thank you for showing my kids a good time at the community center the other day."

"You should enroll them in the afterschool program there. Unless it's a little too urban for your family."

She frowned at him. "You're determined not to like me, aren't you?"

He didn't respond.

"She wasn't right for you. Pumpkin, I mean. She's a dreamer and you're too sensible."

His jaw tensed. Beau didn't expect him to respond. So she was a little surprised when he did.

"Doesn't that disprove your theory of opposites and attraction?"

"I reserve the right to change my mind." She shrugged. "We're more alike than not, you and I. We both enjoy service work. We both like to work with our hands. We both like children."

"But that's where the comparison stops," he said. "Your head is in the clouds and my feet are on the ground."

He stopped walking and faced her. His expression pinched. His long fingers tapped on the Styrofoam cup in his hand.

"Listen, Mrs. Rosen, I will adjust you with my skilled hands which aren't magic. But I put no stock in this dream and true love and The One nonesense."

"So, if you use your skills to adjust me, and I just happen to magically see the face of this woman who's coming towards you in my dreams, you're not interested in knowing her identity?"

He didn't answer. His non-answer was confirmation. He turned and opened the door to the exam room and let her precede him inside.

"Did you get any sleep last night?" he asked.

Beau sighed. "Faunie had a rough night and—"

"You know there's research that suggests you have to let kids learn to self-soothe. If they don't get that skill they'll always rely on you to do everything for them. And that can spread to other facets of their lives."

"Isn't that neglect? Letting a child cry alone in a dark room."

"Neglect of whom? Your children appear well taken care of. It's you who's suffering."

"My children's problems are my problems."

"When do they learn to solve them?"

Beau's hackles went up, but not too far. His voice was gentle, his eyes full of concern for her.

"I'm not saying you're a bad mother. As your doctor I have to insist that you take better care of yourself. You've flown before?"

Beau nodded.

"The stewardess always tells you to put the oxygen mask on yourself first, before you help another person. Otherwise, you both could die. It's the same principle. You have to take care of yourself before you can extend care to another. If you break down, your whole family will break if they don't know how to care for themselves without you."

Beau couldn't deny that she often felt the weight of the world on her shoulders. When she looked around her family, at her own parents, at their surviving siblings and their marriages, they all made their partnerships look so easy and effortless. Their marriages all looked like well-oiled machines that never had any kinks. Sure, she and her cousins acted out in their youth. But all of her family was there to help each other out. Beau wanted to grow the same kind of family.

Dr. Walker reached out his hand to help her onto the adjustment table. There wasn't that spark of electricity between them this time, just a gentle hum.

"I feel like no matter how hard I try at one thing, I fail at another." She didn't know where those words came from. She hadn't even intended to open her mouth. But with her hand in his she couldn't hold the truth in anymore.

"When I do well at my job, my children suffer. When I spend extra time with the kids, my husband is neglected. When I spend time with Faun, Flora gets the short end of the stick. I can't be everything to everyone at all times."

Dr. Walker squeezed her hand. "You should ask for help."

With a gentle nudge he urged her backwards. Beau obliged, thinking to herself that this position, with her prone and this big man over top of her, was strangely intimate. But she trusted Darrell Walker, not only because his strong hands were healing her and bringing her back to herself. She trusted him because his kind eyes saw through her. They saw her pains and discomfort. With gentle pressure, he eased each crick and crack from her body.

"Close your eyes," he said.

She did. She closed her eyes and opened her body to his healing touch. The dream reached out to her almost immediately, but Beau pulled herself back into wakefulness. She caught Dr. Walker's gaze.

"I'll look for you this time," she said.

He raised a quizzical eyebrow as his fingers palpated her neck.

"In my dream, I'll look into the face of the woman meant for you." She closed her eyes again, and immediately fell asleep.

11

———

The last thing that Darrell wanted to do was to admit that he'd been thinking about Beau and her dreams. After she'd left the rec center, he'd sat down with the chess team, and lost to a seventh grader because his mind wasn't in the game.

She'd known about the watch. He couldn't figure out how to explain that. Darrell was a man of science. He knew there had to be an explanation for the coincidence.

But it wasn't a coincidence. The prefix of that word meant it had happened before. It was an incident, singular. He hadn't met Beau Rosen before. Maybe she did have some sort of sixth sense? Maybe the woman in her dreams was the woman of his?

Darrell shook his head at the faulty logic. Beau was in his office not because of the medical reason of easing her pain. She was here because she doubted her own vision of happiness. Was he supposed to believe what she told him about his own love life, if she doubted hers?

Still, he had to admit he was curious as to what she would see now that she'd fallen to sleep. Not that he believed he worked any magic with his hands. He knew that there was energy around the spine. He knew that the right adjustment could relieve any number of maladies. But there were no scientific studies of an adjustment bringing about prophetic visions.

With her eyes closed, Darrell continued to palpate Beau's slim back while she lay facing him. He lifted her torso and used gravity to slip her vertebrae back together. It gave him a moment to study her features.

She had dark, thick tresses. Her olive-tone skin, lighter than Pumpkin's but dark enough to call forth her Mediterranean heritage, reminded him of a dark coffee roast that was heavy with cream.

The thought of Pumpkin made him jerk. It was the first time he'd seen his ex in weeks. The question in her eyes irked him now as it had done since the first time he'd seen her after catching her wrapped around his friend in a coat closet.

"Are you past this yet?" Pumpkin's eyes had asked him.

Gale looked at him with the same version of the question. He hadn't seen Manny in a year. His ex-friend's pale eyes hadn't asked him anything. They all mostly avoided him since the answer to their questions was the same. No, he wasn't past it.

What had stung Darrell the most about Manny's betrayal had been that he wasn't special enough for either of them to stick around for. He couldn't deny that he'd like to be someone's One and Only, someone's fated mate, or star-crossed lover.

Sure, it was a fairytale. Certainly, it was mathematically impossible. But when he looked at Manny and Pumpkin in the society papers, or on local government access channels,

Darrell saw that he had never even been in the running for Pumpkin's heart.

His own father had left him and his mother for another family, leaving behind only that stupid, broken watch. He hadn't chosen Darrell. Darrell wasn't past that yet, either. Because, if he were honest with himself, he would admit that he wanted to be chosen.

Darrell hadn't had many male friends. Many of the guys from the old neighborhood either ignored or jabbed at him for his academic pursuits. They all assumed he'd be good at sports due to his height, but he'd never cared much for ball play. Those pursuits were as much luck as they were physics. Darrell liked things to be precise.

He put his hands on Beau Rosen's back and continued to work at coaxing the nodes of her spine back into place. He placed his hands on the curve of her spine. He closed his eyes and operated through feeling. He was thankful that her gray eyes were closed. In them he saw Manny's grin.

Beau's eyes weren't precisely like Manny's. Her eyes were kind where Manny's were often mischievous. Her eyes were tinted with worry, where Manny rarely had a care in the world.

Beau thought he could do this; heal her and send her into a dream world to identify her husband as the man of her dreams. Her eyes told him so. Looking into those eyes, Darrell wanted to believe it.

He didn't want her to be sad or in pain. He wanted her to feel relief and happiness. He wanted to mend that family where the son was getting all the wrong attention and the daughter was hardly getting any. He wanted to balance out the scales in the family, where the mother carried the weight of a business and a household on her shoulders. He'd yet to see the man of the house. If she had been his wife, Darrell would be at each of these appointments. He'd check in on the progress of his wife's health and healing.

Darrell crossed Beau's arms over her chest. He scooped her up into his arms. She didn't open her eyes, she'd already fallen into a deep sleep. That had never happened to him before in his professional life.

He wondered if his hands were magic? But he chuckled to himself. The huff of air blew a thick curl off Beau's forehead and exposed the baby hairs at her hairline.

Darrell stared at those innocent curls. He felt the weight of her body in his arms. There was a sense of trust in his line of work. The pressure he had to exert on the spine. The sounds the adjustments made. The way he had to contort the body. It all added up to patients being fearful and stiff and hesitant. But not Beau Rosen. No patient had ever given him this kind of trust so soon.

Looking down at her relaxed face, he had the urge to touch those baby hairs at her crown. Instead, he placed his fingers and palms at the appropriate places along her spine. He guided her body back down onto the table and then exerted the necessary pressure to nudge the joints back into place.

He heard the snap, crackle, and pop. She didn't wake. She only sighed. Darrell stared for just a second longer than was professional before he released her from his hold.

He gave her a deep tissue massage to encourage the adjustment to keep its hold. If she wouldn't, or couldn't, take care of herself, it was the least he could do. He let her stay there asleep.

Sliding into the office chair in the exam room, Darrell woke up his phone. There were five notifications from Gage. Scrolling through the potentials with his thumb, he swiped each woman off the list. They were either young coeds or older cougars. One was even outside of the country. Darrell shut his phone off and sighed. On the table, Isabeau Rosen did the same thing.

He wondered what she was seeing in her dreams? Was she confirming the face of her husband? Did she see Darrell in the dream? Did she see someone else, someone coming for him?

Suddenly, Darrell couldn't remember why finding out what she saw was such a bad thing? He knew for a fact that there had never been a divorce in the Charmayne family. And the Charmayne on the table had said that all the couples she saw in her dreams were all still together. Maybe...

As he waited for her to wake up, he became anxious, wondering what she might see, who she might see. Was this dream woman beautiful? Was she smart? Did she want children? Was she local? Would he have to move? How would Beau know her name? Her address? Did she hear their voices in her dreams?

The attraction of having a guarantee suddenly seemed good to him; to be with someone and not worry about them ever leaving. He understood why Beau wanted to be certain of her own happy ending.

Darrell put one hundred percent into everything he did, even the dates he went on. He'd been discouraged when he saw that women didn't give their all, didn't give him a chance. It would be a load off to enter a relationship knowing that it would work out, no matter what.

Twenty minutes later, Beau's eyes fluttered open. It took everything in Darrell not to shake her into wakefulness.

"What did you see?" He was nearly ashamed at the curiosity in his voice. Nearly.

"I didn't." Her face had been relaxed in her repose, but

as she sat up the skin bunched around her eyes. "I didn't see anything." She looked away from him. "I didn't dream. I don't understand?"

Darrell bowed his head. He felt like a fool. He'd let himself get roped into this; another Charmayne fantasy. He stood; his own spine firm and erect. He tugged at his white coat.

"You needed the rest," he said.

He helped her down from the table. The last couple of times he'd taken her hand in his there'd been a spark of electricity between them, which further proved another of the fallacies of this idea of fate and falling in love. This time there was no spark, no magic. Just his capable, skilled hands guiding his patient into wellness.

12

The moment her head hit the pillow later the next night, Beau fell into the dream. Once on familiar ground, she didn't waste time on the roses. She made quick work down the path towards the overlook.

He stood there on the cliff; the man in the gray suit. The man of her dreams. He hadn't begun to turn yet. That was good. Maybe she had time. The dream always ended as he started to turn. Perhaps if she could get to him before he started to turn...

She picked up her bare feet to move towards him. A twinge in her back halted her steps. The second she registered the pain, Darrell was there.

Darrell's hand at the small of her back moved like an eraser on a white board. The pain didn't evaporate as much as it dispersed where his thumb brushed at the base of her spine. With his support, she felt strong, able. She felt like she could fly across the path to the cliff and catch a look at the face of the man of her dreams in no time flat.

With Darrell's help, Beau took a step forward. Before she could lift her second foot, he halted her, pointing behind them. The figure in the distance was coming closer, moving slowly.

Beau knew it was a woman, by the way her hips swayed. She knew that this woman was important by the haze dropping away from her person like a lens coming into focus. Beau felt the ties between this woman and Darrell growing like the vines twining up a tree.

She just wished the woman moved a bit faster. Beau itched to race to the cliff to look into the face of the man she knew had to be her husband, but she'd promised Darrell. She hadn't missed the flash of disappointment that dimmed the corners of his eyes when she awoke from a dreamless sleep after their session. He could deny it all he wanted, but every human being wanted to love and be loved; and the good doctor was no different.

Darrell's dream woman continued to take her time coming into view. Beau chanced a glance behind her at Philip. Oh no. He was turning around. She could nearly make out his profile. She knew she might wake up soon. If she stepped closer she might be able to confirm that it was indeed her husband.

Beau stepped away from Darrell and the oncoming woman. There would be time to turn back. She stepped closer to her dream man. He turned and she saw Philip. It was his face. He was calling her name.

"Beau!"

Beau jerked backwards. Darrell reached for her but she was beyond his reach. She fell.

"Beau, wake up."

Beau opened her eyes. The sun blared through the curtains, backlighting Philip. She blinked rapidly, trying to focus the haze in her eyes. It took a moment before his face came into view. It was the same face as in the dream. Relief flooded her.

"You overslept," Philip frowned. "The kids need their breakfast and they need to get to school."

Beau rubbed at her eyes as he went blurry again. The sun's bright rays weren't helping her focusing issues. If the sun was this bright, it meant the day was well and truly underway.

"You didn't give them anything to eat?" Her voice was as muffled as her eyes were hazy.

Philip blinked at her question, as though trying to puzzle out the words. "Babe, you know I don't cook."

That was true. He usually started his day with a protein shake or a power bar. But there was milk and cereal in the kitchen. How hard could that be?

Beau sat up to argue, but the twinge in her spine beat her mouth to the protest. The breakfast argument slipped down on her totem pole of concern. "Philip, I still can't drive. You'll have to take them to school."

"Beau, I'm already taking over your responsibilities at work. I can't do both."

Her vision cleared in an instant. Her throat made way for sound. She sat up straight in the bed, ignoring her back's disapproval. The twinges in her back loosened the reins she held on her temper. "I do both. I do all every day. I'm asking you for a little help for today."

"So, I'm taking over for you at work, and now you want me to take over for you at home, too."

The blood rushed through Beau's ears. "You act like our children are solely my responsibility."

"No, no, no," he backed away. "Don't try and make me out to be some chauvinist. I've always treated you like an equal. Did I argue when you decided not to stay home with the children?"

Philip's mother still to this day, commented on Beau's out of home activities with disdain. Each morning Beau had to navigate the sneers of the Mom Squad as she drove away from the school and on to work.

"We do the same job and you get equal pay to me." Philip huffed out a breath, reminding her of Faun when she prodded him to clean his room or pick up after himself. "Now we're keeping score?"

Beau had the urge to crawl back under the covers. "No, there's no score. We're on the same side."

He faced her now. His face screwed in frustration. He uncrossed his arms from his chest and reached out to her.

"I'm sorry." He brushed his hands over his face. "We're both under a lot of stress right now. I couldn't do what you do. I couldn't do any of this without you, and it's hard while you're hurt and I'm trying to take it all on. I can't do it by myself."

Philip hung his head. It broke Beau's heart to see him in a position of defeat.

"It's okay," she said. "We'll figure it out."

They had to figure it out. They were in this together. She reached for him. He looked at the clock.

"Damn, I'm going to be late," he said. "Yohance Stanley is coming into the offices today to do a formal evaluation."

Beau's hand fell down onto the mattress. "Philip, I still think you're moving too fast with this consultant."

"With his initial evaluation he identified how we could bring in 50K a month."

That number was astounding. It took Beau and her interns months of calling donors and planning fundraisers to bring in those numbers.

"At that speed we both might be able to take some time off," he said. "Maybe take a vacation."

He leaned into her. Beau looked into his face. The face of the man of her dreams. The sun backlit him. He still had the same boyish good looks, but more mature now.

He leaned in and brushed his lips over hers. His lips were warm. She couldn't remember the last time they'd made love. They had sex, of course. But it was always quick, like they were scratching an itch. She couldn't remember the last time they'd lain in bed looking into each other's eyes, moving slowly, doing the things that drove each of them wild. She wrapped her arms around his neck.

"Hey," he pulled back. "I've got to get to my meeting."

Beau didn't let go. She tried to get closer.

"What's gotten into you?" he asked.

"A good night's sleep." She ran her fingers through his thick hair.

"Yeah, I noticed. No nightmares. Which means I'm not waking up in the middle of the night, either."

"No," she kissed the corner of his mouth. "No nightmares. But I did have a dream. I had *the* dream."

His expression didn't change.

"*The dream.* The one where we met. Don't you remember? We were in the garden and you were in the gray suit."

Philip frowned. "I didn't start wearing gray suits until you started buying them for me. Besides, we met at the Henderson's beach house and I'm sure I was in board shorts."

"Philip, I told you this a million times."

Well, maybe not a million. She'd broached the subject of her visions with him, but he thought it funny, and then weird. So, they hadn't talked much about them. And soon after, when she got pregnant, she stopped having the visions all together. She hadn't needed them anymore. She'd found her dream man.

"It doesn't matter." He squirmed out of her embrace. "Crap, now I'm going to be late. And the kids are going to be late, too, if you don't get up."

"Can't you take them? They're on your way into the office."

"It always messes with my schedule when I take them. Plus, their car seats left an impression in my leather interior the last time."

"Dr. Walker said I shouldn't drive."

"What does he know? He's a chiropractor, not a real doctor." Philip's phone rang. "That's Stanley. Listen, I gotta go, babe." He dashed out of the room in his black suit.

Beau stared out the open bedroom door.

She reached for the phone to call Darrell's office. She was surprised when she heard his voice on the other end of the line.

"Hey, Dr. Darrell. It's Beau, Beau Rosen."

"Good morning, Mrs. Rosen."

"I didn't expect you to pick up your phone."

"My receptionist has a late morning because I'm due at an event across town. How are you feeling this morning?"

"I'm feeling well, thank you." Beau rolled her neck. "I had a good night's sleep. You're better than Ambien."

"Magic hands give better hallucinations than that drug," he said.

Beau opened her mouth to respond. Then closed it as she ran his words over in her head.

"That was supposed to be a joke," he said. "I need to stop attempting those. They always seem to come out creepy."

Beau laughed at that. Not at his failed attempt at humor.

She laughed at his self-deprecation. Pumpkin was right about him being awkward, but Beau was finding it charming. She could see how it might put some women off, that he wasn't a smooth operator. But he was genuine. Suddenly Beau shared Pumpkin's hope that Darrell found someone special for himself. And then she remembered.

"Oh crap!" She slapped her hand against her forehead. "I am the worst person."

"What's the matter?" he asked.

"I didn't turn back around."

"I'm not following?"

"In my dream. I had the dream again. It was my husband, by the way. It was Philip who turned around and I saw his face."

There was a pause. She knew Darrell didn't put any stock in her visions, much like her husband apparently.

"I'm glad that cleared things up for you," he said.

"You were there again. You helped me up, helped me to stand and take a step forward. You pointed to a woman in the distance. She was coming closer. If I'd turned back around before waking up I would've seen her. But I didn't. I was too concerned with making sure it was Philip standing there on the cliff. I'm so sorry, Darrell."

"Mrs. Rosen, it's perfectly all right."

"But you deserve your own happily-ever-after. Don't you want to know who your dream woman is?"

He hesitated. Then, "This is not an appropriate conversation to have with a patient."

"You've been in my dreams. I think we've passed appropriate." Beau chuckled. Then the words that came out of her mouth replayed in her head. It seemed that both of them should cease their attempts at jokes today. "Listen, all

I'm saying is that you've been helping me with my problems. I don't see why I can't help you with yours."

"I don't have a problem."

"Have you found The One yet on that dating app of yours?"

Silence from the other end of the line.

"I almost saw her. When I have another dream I'll be sure to turn around and look. I promise."

She heard the hesitation in his silence.

"You know magic works, Darrell. Just look at Manny and—"

God she couldn't stop putting her foot in her mouth.

"There's someone out there for you," she tried again. "I saw her coming towards you. She's almost here. She's so close."

"Is that why you're calling me?"

"No, I was calling to see if I could push my appointment back? I have to get the kids to school and I'm already running late."

"Were you planning on driving?"

"Well... my husband couldn't get them to school because..." She didn't want to say he was busy. She already got the sense that Darrell didn't approve of Philip's parenting style. Most of her family didn't approve of him, but they just hadn't gotten the chance to get to know him better these six years.

"You really shouldn't be driving. Can't you call someone to help you?"

Beau hesitated. She was so used to doing things on her own. "I could probably just call a cab or an Uber. Parish Academy isn't that far from where I live."

"Parish Academy? That's where I'm headed. I'm doing a career day talk with the students."

Beau had forgotten about that. She'd told the PTA that she had been in an accident and would need to reschedule her talk.

"Give me your address," said Dr. Darrell. "I'll come and get you all."

"You don't have to do that."

"I can't have you getting in another car accident before you go back to sleep and wake to tell me all about this dream woman of mine, now can I?"

Beau grinned. "No, I guess not." She gave him her address.

13

"But if your back is broken won't you be dead?"

"No, Eddie. Dr. Darrell pats people on the back who are choking. Isn't that right, Dr. Darrell?"

Darrell smiled down at the children as they tried to make sense of his career. He looked out at all the curious and confused faces. "Actually, Alice, some people who break their backs do go on to live. But they might get confined to a wheel chair. Or they might get prosthetic legs."

"You mean like my Uncle Charlie?" said Eddie. "He was a soldier and now he has only one real leg and the other is a metal thing like an ice cream scoop. He can run really fast. Faster than my dad. He's part robot now."

"And, Alice," Darrell turned to the young girl who had a frown on her brow that she'd been proven wrong by not one but two boys. "I do pat people on their backs and help them to feel better."

Alice smiled, vindicated.

"He patted my mommy on the back and she fell asleep."

A pair of gray-blue eyes looked up at him in hero worship. Flora Rosen held her head high and proud.

Darrell looked over in the corner at Flora's mother. Beau smiled back at him. Darrell ignored the flutter that skittered over his fingertips at the memory of palpating the woman's spine. He'd worked on countless women's spines over the years. But it was strange; he knew that if he closed his eyes he'd feel every node and dip of Beau Rosen's back.

"Did it hurt?" Eddie addressed his question to Beau.

Beau stepped forward. "No, it didn't hurt. It felt…"

Darrell waited for the adjective, strangely anxious to know how she'd characterize his services.

"It felt like a big sigh of relief."

Darrell continued explaining things to the kids of the Kindergarten class. Children, he got. Children got him. It was grown adults that he often had problems relating to.

"But it sounds dangerous," said Alice. "What if you make a mistake?"

"I studied really hard in school to make sure that I don't make any mistakes," Darrell assured her. "But if I do make a mistake, I apologize and then I fix it."

"Can I get a justment?" asked Eddie.

Darrell nodded. "Children's bodies are pretty flexible."

"Like Elasti-Girl?"

Darrell grinned. He was once again on familiar turf. "Yes, like Elasti-Girl. And children heal faster than adults, like Wolverine."

The kids cheered at the comparison to the superheroes.

"Chiropractors don't just specialize in the back. We work on all joints. Do you know what a joint is?"

"Yeah, my dad rolls them—"

"Kenny," Ms. McFagden, their teacher's assistant stepped forward with a stern look that shut the kid up. She smiled apologetically at Darrell, pushing a lock of hair that had not gone astray behind her ear and looking up at him from under her eyelashes.

Darrell didn't mind the interruption. He knew kids were precocious. "A joint is when one bone connects to the other. For example, your head is connected to your shoulders by your neck."

He rolled his neck and the children followed suit.

"Or your wrist, or hands, knees and feet."

He rotated each joint in turn causing the children to wiggle in their seats as they repeated the actions.

"I can crack my knuckles," said Eddie. "Could I be a chiropractice?"

"I bet you could be a chiropractor," Darrell smiled. "So, as you see, chiropractors help people when their bodies don't feel one-hundred percent."

Ms. McFagden led the children in a round of applause for his presentation. "All right, every one line up for recess."

Darrell watched the children line up. Flora ran to her mother and reached up to give her a hug. Beau patted her daughter on the head while she looked off at her sullen son.

Mrs. Knighting thanked Darrell and then followed the children outside to recess. Ms. McFadgen lingered behind, coming up to Darrell.

"That was a fantastic presentation." She pushed the same lock of hair, the one that was perfectly placed, behind her ear again. "You know, I've been having all kinds of problems sleeping."

"Seems to be going around." Darrell looked up at Beau who hung back at the wall, not joining them.

"Maybe that's something you could help me with?" The aide pushed a different lock of hair behind her ear. She blinked her eyes a couple of times.

Darrell wondered if it was more than insomnia that ailed her. Maybe she had dandruff or an itchy scalp bothering her too. He'd have to check her out and give her a full evaluation before making any snap judgements.

"Sure," he pulled out a card. "Just give my office a call and set up an appointment. I accept all insurance." He smiled at Ms. McFadgen and then turned to Beau. He had to get back to the office soon. "Are you ready, Mrs. Rosen?"

Beau Rosen looked between him and Ms. McFagden. Then she shook her head and preceded him out the door.

"No wonder you're hopeless at dating," she said once they were out of the school. "You don't even know when a woman is hitting on you."

"What are you talking about?"

"Never mind. I'll take it from here." She ducked through the car door that he held open for her, into the passenger seat. She tossed her bag into the back with her children's car seats.

"My Aunt Gale would say we're on the same karass," she said as they headed towards his office.

"The Egyptian boat that carries souls."

"Not a lot of people know that."

"Not a lot of people are history nerds," he said. "I've been fascinated with Egyptian history since I was a kid. All the physical wonders they accomplished without the help of modern machinery."

Beau looked at him with... was that amusement? He often had trouble determining if women were actually amused or just pretending.

"You have the same wide-eyed wonder as Pumpkin's son, Seth." She propped her elbow on the car door and rested her cheek on her balled fist.

"He's a smart kid. Reminds me of myself at that age. Just me and my mom and tons of books."

"Did your father abandon your mother, too?"

Darrell gave a curt nod.

"Did he come back, like Seth's dad?"

"No, he has another family now. One he likes better."

"I'm sorry."

Darrell shrugged. "It's not your fault."

"Is that why you work with kids?"

He shrugged again. "I guess part of me wants to be a model for my gender, let kids know that all men aren't bad. My mother was in love with my father. She never got over him leaving. Never dated anyone else. She always waited for him to come back. I think she's still waiting, in fact. By your logic, he's her true love. But she isn't his. How do you account for that?"

Beau had no answer.

"I understand your need to be certain of the magic," he continued. "But I think math and logic are more certain than a dream. I think people should have things in common, be compatible before they decide to spend their lives together. If they only work off of love, or lust, they won't stick it out. Is there anything wrong with making sure the foundation is secure before you start to build?"

"No," she said. "But I still think you need that spark to begin with. I still think that passion is important in a relationship."

"I think you're a people-pleaser," he said, as he pulled into his office parking lot.

"Is there something wrong with liking to see people happy?"

"When it takes away your own happiness, then yes."

"I'm happy," she insisted.

He stared at her for a moment, then he reached for the door handle. "Let's get you flat on your back."

Beau blinked.

"I mean on the table for your adjustment. So you can slip into your magic dream world and find me a princess."

14

Beau fell into the dream. She couldn't tell if it was her imagination —well she was in her head so wasn't this her imagination? But everything seemed brighter, clearer. The flowers were redder, the grass greener.

She saw Philip in the distance. Standing looking out across the sky in his gray suit. The light played a trick on her eyes making the suit appear a darker shade of gray. Or perhaps, was that blue?

Beau blinked. She braced for the slough to fog over her, for her feet to be weighed down. But it didn't. They weren't.

It was easier for her to stand up. She didn't feel a hand on her back but she sensed him near. She turned to see Darrell. He stood tall, smiling down at her. It wasn't his professional smile. It was the smile she'd coaxed from him earlier. The genuine smile; one he might give to a friend.

There was a gleam in his eyes as he looked at her. She felt strengthened by it. He gave her a slight nod and she straightened on her own. His smile deepened.

She looked over his shoulder to see the woman, the

woman of his dreams, coming closer. She wasn't close enough yet to make out her features.

Beau turned to look behind her, at the man of her dreams. Philip was walking away. He'd never done that before. She knew she was supposed to follow Philip. She always followed Philip. She was always there when he made a misstep or when he felt the harsh weight of disappointment. That's what marriage was all about; lending one another support.

Beau prepared to take a step toward her partner. She knew she had to hurry to catch up to him, to see where the next part of this dream led them. She raised her foot, but when it hit the ground, she stumbled.

Darrell was there in an instant. He gripped her shoulder with one hand and brought his soothing, healing touch to the base of her spine with the other. Their gazes locked.

His pupils dilated, the black irises overtook the brown like a rose unfurling its bloom. Beau leaned back and found herself caught in his gaze, in his embrace. It had been so long since she'd been held; really held, where she trusted that her partner would take her weight and not let her fall.

She knew she should break away from this man and go to her husband. But she had no desire to be anywhere but here. Darrell's hold on her wasn't improper. In the center of those intelligent eyes grew care and concern. For her. Darrell's eyes reminded her of her father's eyes.

Lionel Rumpel was the gentlest spirit Beau had ever known. He was also fiercely protective. Beau could tell her father anything. She spent countless hours sitting quietly and contently in the cradle of her father's barrel chest, where it was safe and warm.

An ache of longing washed over her as Darrell steadied her back on her feet. She hadn't spent much time with her father over the past few years. There was often tension on his visits. Her father and Philip did not see eye to eye where the care of his daughter was concerned. Lionel held his tongue, but Beau saw his disapproval in the furrowing of his soft blue eyes.

Beau caught movement over Darrell's shoulder. The woman of his dreams was coming into view. Not stepping out of Darrell's warm embrace, Beau craned to see the woman moving slowly towards them.

Darrell stood by her side, patiently waiting. Beau was not patient. She believed everyone should have a happily-ever-after. Darrell was so kind and giving of his time, he deserved to have the same returned to him. And she wanted to be the one to present it to him. She took a step forward.

Finally the other woman's face came into view. Beau had to squint. She looked vaguely familiar. She hadn't considered that; that she might not know this person. At least she'd be able to give Darrell a description of who the woman was. Dark hair—was that chestnut, or maybe auburn, she couldn't be sure? Light eyes, maybe hazel, maybe green? Her figure was wavy, or maybe she was curvy. She appeared shorter than Beau, but most women were.

The woman moved faster now. Even though she came nearer, she didn't become clearer. Beau reached out to grab for her, but the woman went through her hands like a ghost. The woman headed towards the skyline that Philip had been moving towards.

Philip.

Beau turned back to see Philip fading into the skyline.

She turned back to tell Darrell that she had to go. He still stood there, solid and firm. She reached out to him but her own body was fading, slipping through his grasp.

She woke up with a start.

Dr. Darrell Walker sat at a small desk in the exam-room reading a book. He reminded her of a sentinel keeping watch. His spectacled eyes peered over the top of the pages. He gave her the professional smile. Disappointment rained down her spine at the polite uptilt of his lips.

"How long have I been out?" she asked.

"A couple of hours." He marked his place in the book and placed it on the desk.

"Oh, god, have I kept you?"

"No, I just finished with my last patient about twenty minutes ago. I wanted you to rest." His eyes softened to that cool, warm, brown of the earth. "It looks like you haven't been getting enough."

"So, you were looking out for my well-being?"

"Of course," he frowned. "What else would I be doing?"

"Waiting to see if I saw your dream woman."

"I want you to be well."

He came to her and helped her to a sitting position. When his palm came to grasp under her elbow, Beau felt the same sunny warmth shine throughout her body. She rested her hand on his strong bicep and allowed him to pull her up. Once she was sitting upright, he let her go.

"You need to take better care of yourself," he said. "You need to enlist the help of your family to do so. I tried calling your husband to have him come and pick you up. He's listed as your emergency contact. But his office said he's out and wasn't taking any forwarding calls."

"He has a big meeting today."

Beau knew he wanted to say more. But he didn't.

"I saw her," she offered. "The woman of your dreams... in my dream." She didn't imagine that his ears perked up. Even though his face remained a cool mask. "Don't you want to know about her?"

He opened his mouth and then closed it.

"She had dark hair and light eyes. I'm sure she was beautiful."

"I don't care about things like that."

"Physical beauty usually matters to guys."

"It's not even on my list."

"You have a list?"

He didn't answer.

"I think her hair might've been red, not brown."

He raised an eyebrow at that. With Darrell being African-American she wondered if he'd dated across cultural lines. Her own family was a hodgepodge of ethnicities.

"She did have light-colored eyes, though. But I couldn't tell if they were light brown or green. She was hazy, like a ghost. She was shorter than you."

"Everyone's shorter than I am."

Beau smiled and Darrell smiled back; the genuine smile. The smile he'd give to a friend.

"You deserve to be happy, Darrell. Everyone who meets you seems to believe so."

She saw him stiffen and close off. His eyes hardened and his smile turned cool and professional.

"You don't seem to be able to see that people are interested in you," she continued. "I saw a woman who is your ideal mate. I don't know her name, but I know that if I saw her in reality I could identify her. Don't you want a guarantee?"

He sighed. But it wasn't a sigh of annoyance. It was resignation. She grinned, she was wearing him down.

Beau checked the time. Normally she'd be in her office fielding calls and writing grant proposals, but she had different charity work she wanted to do today. "What are you about to do? Can I take you to lunch?"

"I have to go to check in at the community center. The Director is out on maternity leave and I'm lending a hand."

"I'll come with you."

Darrell was quiet on the drive over. Beau couldn't engage him in conversation, so she simply chatted. She relaxed in his car. The last thing she wanted to do was go home and sit. She was far too much of a busy body to ever be idle.

The kids didn't need to be picked up from school for a couple of hours more. Philip never returned home from work before six in the evening. She would've gone into the office, but being out and about was such a welcome change from sitting at a desk on the phone all day long. Or working her way through a social gathering.

They pulled up to the community center. The face of the building needed a new paint job. Beau made a mental note to see who funded the venture. It was likely a government-funded center.

"Hey, Dr. D," said a teen with a basketball in his hand. His clothes were shabby and his face unwashed.

"Aren't you supposed to be in school?" Darrell asked.

"It's a holiday." The kid said with a cheeky grin.

"Let me guess? A holiday that only you celebrate."

"You got it, Dr. D." The kid continued down the hall.

Beau stared after him. "Aren't you gonna call his school or his parents?"

Darrell shook his head. "There's no one at home to call. He might be on out-of-school suspension. It's better he's in here than on the streets."

Beau followed Darrell to an outside courtyard. She looked over to a chain link fence and saw an overrun garden. "What's this?"

Darrell turned back. Beau had stopped, so he'd gotten a few feet away from her. "It was an organization's attempt at a garden."

"It didn't work?"

"Charity organizations don't tend to stick around here."

The garden was overrun, but she saw tomatoes and vegetables.

"Mrs. Paulson, I thought you were still on maternity leave."

Beau looked up to see Darrell embrace a woman about their age. Her hair was done in intricate braids. She wore a colorful pattern that called to the tribes of an African culture.

"I just started back to work today. I miss my baby already."

Beau understood that. When she put the kids in daycare two years ago she cried in the car for an hour before pulling herself together to leave the school parking lot and head into work.

"Paulson?" Beau said. "Are you by any chance related to a Stefan Paulson?"

The woman nodded. "And you're Isabeau Rosen. I directed my husband to you after all of the great work you did with Charmayne Foundation."

"I've been trying to figure out how to help him."

"Our community really needs it," said Mrs. Paulson. "I'm sure you know the parish has taken in many refugees over the last few years."

Beau had not known. She'd been so focused on international matters that she hadn't seen how close they'd hit home.

"The boys are getting pulled into wars," said Mrs. Rosen. "But the girls suffer too. And not just from Africa and the

Middle East. We have girls from South America who have met with strife. They are so scarred, inside and out. They are smart but I'm trying to get them to see all that they have to gain in America. You don't have to solely be someone's wife or mother. You can be more."

Beau had always believed that. She'd always known she was destined to be a mother. But she'd wanted a career too. Luckily for these girls, her career afforded her the opportunity to help improve their lives.

"Mrs. Paulson," she said, "can we go inside and talk?"

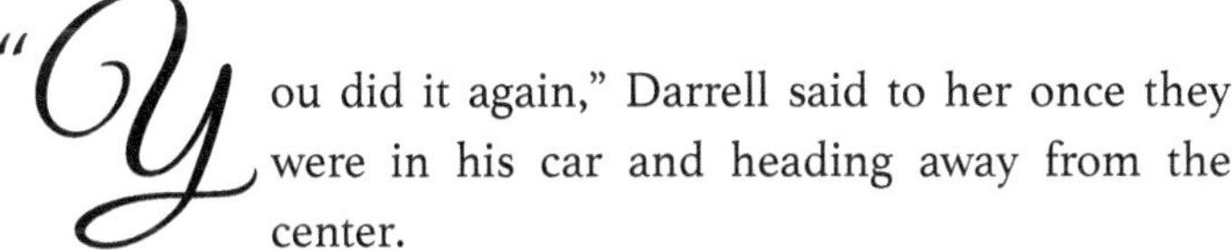

15

"You did it again," Darrell said to her once they were in his car and heading away from the center.

"Did what?" Beau stretched her arms over her head in the passenger seat. She rolled her neck and winced.

Darrell's hands itched to get at the crick that offended the perfection of her spine.

He shook himself. *Perfection of her spine?* Did he really just think that? Clearly he was spending too much time around Mrs. Isabeau Rosen. Her head-in-the-clouds ideals were seeping into his rational brain.

"You took on more responsibilities," he said.

In the span of time it had taken Darrell to go into the volunteer office and add the dates of the upcoming chess match to the calendar, Mrs. Paulson and Beau decided they would hold a debutante cotillion for the refugee, displaced, and economically disadvantaged children of the community.

"It's not exactly a cotillion." She twisted excitedly in the car seat as they headed back to the elementary school.

"There will be dancing, but it will be cultural dancing. Many of the girls are from West Africa, so there will be traditional African dancing and drumming. There are also refugees from Bolivia. I didn't even know there was a war going on in Bolivia. So there will be Bolivian folk dancing. I want to make sure every culture will be represented."

She bounced in her seat like a little girl. It reminded him of little Flora.

"There will be aspects of a cotillion, but more like a debutante ball because I want their fathers or brothers to walk the girls out and present them to society."

"Like a beauty pageant?" he said.

"What's wrong with that?" She frowned at him as though he'd deflated her balloon of enthusiasm.

Darrell shrugged. "I guess I didn't expect to hear that from a modern woman. My experience has been that today's women want to be treated as equals. They want you to see their brains and personality, before you see their beauty."

"Women are very complex creatures. We want it all."

"Tell me about it. My mother had to do it all and was never regarded as equal. She thought feminists were entitled women who didn't know what it meant to have to take care of a child, a house, a job, and a man."

"And what do you think?"

Darrell couldn't tell if she was annoyed at his stance on this topic, or impressed that he'd thought about the plight of female autonomy. "I'm a scientist. True equality is impossible; especially in a human partnership. I believe each partner should step in when they're needed. In that case, it will never be exactly equal."

She stared at him without saying anything.

"But," he proceeded, "I've also seen people, men and

women, who take on more than they can manage. When the scales tip, the person who's taken on more than their load typically falls." He gave her a pointed glance.

"I took the day off work," she protested. "I'm in the passenger seat."

"But you just took on a large project."

She made a *pfft* sound with her lips and waved his words away. "I used to plan things like this all the time when I worked for the Charmayne Foundation. I'm the daughter of a debutante, and I had my own ball. This cotillion will be a walk in the park."

"I imagine the Charmayne Foundation has a much larger work force than the Rosen Foundation?" Darrell explicitly meant her absentee husband.

"The Charmayne's are a large clan."

Darrell had never met them all when he and Manny were friends. Only less than half of them, and he couldn't keep them all straight. It had only ever been his mother and him.

"My family is around to lend a hand if I ask. That's what families do. And friends," she smiled at him.

Darrell was caught off-guard by that smile. Beau's smile was so much like her cousin's; open and inclusive. It said, I have a secret and I'll only share it with you. For a moment, just a few seconds, he found himself missing Manny Charmayne.

Darrell had met Manny at a house party. He'd felt completely out of place and hadn't known anyone. Manny had stood next to him, asking another man a question. He'd turned to Darrell, a perfect stranger at the time, for confirmation. Darrell had agreed with Manny and even attempted a joke. The joke went wrong, of course.

Manny's companion had frowned at Darrell, but Manny

had laughed and clapped Darrell on the shoulder. Darrell hadn't said much more for the rest of the night, but Manny had continued to include him in the conversations as though they were old friends. And from that point they were.

Until they weren't.

An image of Manny and Pumpkin locked together in a closet came to mind. It didn't hurt as much as it had for the last year. Another image came to his mind. Pumpkin's face when she'd tried to apologize. And then her face each time he'd seen her at the community center to pick up her son. She always made a point to say hello to him, to check on him. She never pushed him, but she always seemed to be waiting. As though she were waiting for him to resume their friendship. But why did she care about him when she had what she wanted; Manny.

Manny had tried to apologize exactly once. The image of Manny popped into his head from the last time he'd seen him. The man whom he had called his friend hadn't looked smug. He'd looked... sad. There had been a plea in his voice.

Anthony had abandoned Pumpkin, but she and Seth had forgiven him. The two were working towards a new kind of relationship. Could there be a chance for Darrell to forgive Manny? A chance for them to rebuild their friendship?

Darrell shut the thought down. Friends didn't steal from other friends. They didn't betray them.

He looked again at Beau. They weren't friends. They had a business relationship and it had already gone beyond the professional.

"Make sure your family and friends help you with this," he said.

"Oh, you're helping," she said.

Darrell opened his mouth to protest. They weren't friends. Beau raised an eyebrow, as though daring him to deny their relationship.

His words got lost in the arch of that eyebrow. His protest burned in the twinkle in her light eyes. He shut his mouth when his gaze got caught at the uptilt to her lush lips.

She turned away from him and prattled on about her plans and his role in them. He meant to tell her no. He meant to set the boundary that they were only doctor and patient.

For some reason, he let her keep talking. She began using the word 'we.' She kept asking his opinions. And then she would incorporate his responses into her plans.

He gave up the protest, but he was able to gain one concession. "I think your husband should take on some of these responsibilities."

Beau looked out the window. "I'll talk to him about it tonight."

"You two have been married for..."

"Six years."

Darrell did the math in his head. The twins were five.

She frowned at him as though she knew what he was thinking. "It was love at first sight."

"I thought the first time you saw him was in a dream?"

She grinned; huge and bright as the sun. "We..." she began and then she paused. "Well, there's some dispute on how we met. Philip and I remember it differently. We met at a beach house. But he thinks we met when he came back from the beach. I think we met at a party when he was dressed in a gray suit."

"What difference does that make?"

"It doesn't," she said. "Not really. The point is we're

together now, and we're happy. I got pregnant shortly after we met. But like I said, I knew he was The One. So, it wasn't irresponsible. It was inevitable. And he did the right thing, not because he's a gentleman—which he is. But because he loved me. *Loves* me."

"I'm not challenging you."

"I didn't say you were."

"You seem a bit defensive."

"Everything's fine," she insisted. "It's just that everything's so busy with work. And we have the twins."

"Are you saying that the romance is gone?"

"We don't have time for romance. Not with twins and a business to run. I'm sure when the kids are older and the business is solid, we'll have more time for each other. I look at Pumpkin for an example. Now that Seth is ten, she and Manny have tons of time to spend together."

Darrell noted that that statement didn't sting like it might have a few weeks ago. "You don't want any more children?"

"I did." Beau looked out the window. "But two are a handful."

Darrell wondered if those were actually her words, or her husband's.

"That's why I want to find someone compatible," he said. "The honeymoon phase fades. Then you're left with a normal person. I want to make sure I like that person."

"I like Philip."

Darrell decided to ignore the hitch in her voice. "Because you two have a lot in common?"

"We have enough things in common." She hesitated. "But then, there are things we differ on. You don't just want a carbon copy of yourself."

"That's a good point," Darrell agreed.

They pulled up to the school. Darrell parked. When Beau reached for the door handle, he frowned.

"What are you doing?" he said.

"Getting out of the car," she said with confusion.

"A gentleman always opens the door for a lady."

She sat back in her seat and he came around the other side.

As he rounded the car he noted a red-haired woman getting out of her car. The redhead smiled politely at him.

Darrell paused, thinking on Beau's words about a dark-haired woman, who could've had chestnut or red hair, with light eyes, that could've been hazel or brown. This woman was short. She had a shapely, curvy figure.

"It's you," Beau said from behind him.

Darrell looked down at Beau who'd opened the car door and was stepping out.

"Darrell, it's her," Beau insisted.

"Who's me?" The woman asked.

"Duchess, right? We met the other day. I want you to meet my friend, Darrell."

16

"When are you going to ask her out?" Beau hedged.

She'd had to maneuver the exchange of phone numbers between Darrell and Duchess. The two grown adults had been as awkward as middle schoolers trying to arrange plans for their first afterschool dance.

In the driver's seat, Darrell kept his hands on the wheel and his eyes on the road, steadily ignoring her. His hands were at ten and two, his chair erect. His phone was plugged into the hands free system.

"Where are you going, mommy?" Flora bounced in her car seat.

"I'm not going anywhere, sweetie. Dr. Darrell is. He's going on a date."

"Can I go on a date with you, Dr. Darrell?"

Darrell tore his gaze from the road and glanced in the rearview mirror. His carefully blank veneer cracked a smile at Flora. It was the friendly smile.

"I would like that," he said. "We can go on a date to the rec center when your mother has her cultural cotillion."

"Cultural Cotillion," Beau mused. "I just love the sound of that."

Darrell ignored her and kept his attention on Flora. "There's going to be a part where you walk out on a stage. Maybe your dad can walk with you?"

Flora's face fell from beaming bright to dull disappointment. "My daddy is busy. He works a lot at the gym in the morning. Then at golf while we're at school. Then he works at his club at night. He probably can't make it."

Beau opened her mouth to protest, but no words came to her husband's defense. She couldn't remember the last time they'd all done something as a family. Philip had never taken Flora or Faun out for one-on-one time. Even though Beau was a twin, each of her parents made time for both her brother and her —together and separately.

"Then you can be my date," Darrell offered. "That means I'll be walking with the prettiest girl in the whole city."

Flora smiled as though Darrell had offered her a shopping spree in a toy store.

Darrell's eyes shifted in the rear view mirror. "Are you gonna come, too, Faun?" Darrell asked.

Faun looked up beneath hooded eyes, suspiciously. "Dates are for girls."

Darrell nodded at these sage words. "That's true. Girls like to go on dates. Men, like you and me, prefer to hangout. Maybe we could hangout while Flora gets ready for our date. You know girls take forever to get ready."

"They do," agreed Faun. "Flora is in the bathroom for hours and hours in the morning. But I think it's 'cause she has to sit down and I stand up."

Darrell nodded again. "Well, that will give us time to hang out. What do you say?"

"Sure," Faun shrugged. "That would be okay."

Faun went back to looking out the window, but he was less sulky. Flora sang a tune from the Disney Channel. Darrell went back to eyeing the road, but his smile lingered.

"You do realize you just reinforced gender stereotypes to my two, impressionable children," Beau said.

"They were true statements. It does take women longer to get ready because they sit down. Whereas, men stand."

He took his eyes off the road. His face was stoic with scholarly assurance. But she caught the quiver at the corner of his mouth. She laughed first, and he followed suit.

Darrell's laugh was deep, as if it came from a place locked inside the core of him. The tip of it was hollow, but then it filled with resonance as it made its way up and out of his chest. His cheeks creased as he smiled. His brown eyes sparkled with light. Darrell Walker's momentary happiness shifted something inside of her.

"Are you gonna answer my other question?" she asked.

Darrell sighed, but his eyes stayed soft and a hint of the smile remained. Being in love would keep the light shining bright in his eyes. It would ease the creakiness of his unused smile.

"She's perfect for you," Beau insisted.

"You barely know this woman," he said.

"I don't have to *know* her to know. You get to know her and tell me I'm right. I've never been wrong."

"You're gonna nag me until I ask her out, aren't you?"

"Another stereotype, but it happens to be true. I will nag you until you ask Duchess out. Then I will nag you until you confirm that I am right about the two of you."

"Nag," he mused. "You know that word's origin is Germanic. It refers to a small horse. But in Scandanavian it means to naw at."

"I know what you're doing," Beau said. "You're trying to distract me with your intellect."

"Bore you actually. Is it working?"

"Not in the least."

Darrell turned to her, giving her a full, friendly smile. Beau's heart warmed as though the sun shined on it directly. It made her feel warm and safe.

Darrell had been in her dreams. Whenever anyone entered her dream garden, they became a part of her family. Darrell Walker was now her family; whether he wanted it or not.

"You're sure about this?" he asked, as he turned onto her street.

Beau's heart skipped a beat when she saw a glimmer of hope in his eyes. She wanted to be right. She'd been right about everyone, even if she'd had a few doubts about her own dream man. But those doubts were now dismissed. She nodded in affirmation at Darrell.

"Then I'll ask her out," he conceded.

Beau became irrationally excited about the prospect of the date. She wanted to talk with Darrell about what he'd wear, topics of conversation to have, and to avoid, with Duchess. But she held herself back. For now. She could nag him some more over dinner. Her mind pulled up a visual picture of what she had in the fridge that she could prepare.

The car came to a stop before she'd finished planning the menu. She realized, with some disappointment, that they were at her home. Philip's car was in the driveway.

"My husband's home. He's never home this early."

"Good." Darrell put the car in park. "Maybe he's made dinner."

Beau snorted a laugh. Philip didn't even know where the kitchen was in their house.

Darrell got out of the car. He came around to Beau's side first and let her out. Then he went to the back to help Flora out.

Flora bounded into his arms with glee and Darrell gave her another genuine laugh as he set her on her feet. He didn't open Faun's door. He let the boy do it himself while he watched out of the corner of his eye.

"You want to come in and meet my husband?" Beau asked.

"Maybe some other time. I have a call to make, remember."

"Yes, you do. Maybe we can all double date in the near future?"

"We'll see."

They stood awkwardly before each other. Beau had thrust herself upon him. She had no doubt they were going to be a part of each other's lives from this day forward. But they were still in that becoming-friends stage. It wouldn't be appropriate to give him the hug she wanted to. So she reached out and rubbed his shoulder. A spark of static cling caught her.

"Sorry about that," said Darrell. "It seems to keep happening between us."

"You'll let me know what Duchess says?"

"Do I have a choice?" He rounded the car back to the driver's side. "I'm half worried that you'll turn up on the date and coach us through."

Beau raised her eyebrows to consider this. Darrell ducked into the car shaking his head. She waved as he pulled off. Then she and the children turned to enter their home.

It was tough to push the front door open. She had to give it a good shove. There was something blocking the way.

Beau got the door open and saw mountains of boxes in the foyer and living room.

"Philip?"

"In the office, babe."

Beau sent the children to their room and picked her way around the boxes to the home office. Philip sat behind the desk with a stack of papers in his hands. His face screwed in concentration.

"Philip? What's going on? Why are there boxes all over the place?"

"Those are from the office. I decided to close it."

"You what?"

"The interns never show up. We were wasting money with the overhead. With the money we save from letting go of the lease alone, we'll save a fortune."

"You closed the office?" Beau couldn't tell if she was shouting or whispering. The ringing in her ears was so loud. He couldn't be serious.

Evidently she must have shouted. Philip's brows drew in and he crossed his arms over his chest. "You kept making snide comments about how much work you do, how you do more than your fair share. Not only did I take away half of your workload, but I made it so you don't have to leave the house. Isn't that what you wanted?"

Beau's head spun. She wasn't sure which way was up and which way was down. Where was left and was he right? "You should've talked with me about this first."

"Partners trust each other," he said. "You don't trust me?"

That petulant lip, so much like his son's, quivered. It wrenched Beau's heart.

"Our goal is to make money for the less fortunate," he continued. "We make phone calls and go to events. We were spending money on an office that wasn't necessary to run our business. It was a waste."

Beau fixated on that word *we*. Philip had never made a donor phone call in his life. He was rarely in the office. And when they did go to events, she was the one who did most of the schmoozing, while he sulked in a corner. All that aside, she had to admit the office was an extra expense that they were barely able to afford with the foundation's income.

"Okay, maybe you're right," she said. "But you still should've talked with me about it before taking action."

"I'm talking to you now."

"Where will our staff sit? In the living room?"

"I got rid of the staff too. Only one of them even showed up the past two days. We don't need them either."

Beau had to sit down. That word *we* was whistling loudly in her ears. She'd hired the interns when the office work had become too overwhelming for her.

"Stanley said we don't need them," Philip was saying. "His firm has people at their offices. They now work for us, calling up potential donors. I've trimmed so much money off our overhead. All that's left is our salaries and the consultant fees. Not only are we going to save money by what we've cut, we're going to make more money with Stanley's firm. This is a great idea."

Philip shoved aside a box that was in his way. Beau noted that none of them were marked to indicate what the contents were. It was going to take forever for them to unpack and reorganize everything.

"I figure you can file those when you have a second," he said. "You know I'm no good at filing and paperwork. Plus, I'm going to an event Stanley's hosting tonight. So I wouldn't have time anyway."

But she did? He'd just made these life-altering decisions that affected not only her, but they affected the people who had worked for them, and the people they helped. Now he was dumping it on her and leaving. Beau hated fighting with her husband, but this called for a serious tongue-lashing. She opened her mouth to begin.

But Faun entered the room. "Hey dad, Flora's in the bathroom. She's gonna be forever, cause she's a girl. I was wondering if you wanna hang out? You know, like guys?"

"Not now, buddy. Daddy's got a meeting."

Philip barely glanced at the boy as he made his way around the boxes. A few sheets of paper fluttered to the floor as he left out of the room. Faun put his sulking frown back into place and stalked out of the room, leaving Beau behind to pick up the pieces of paper.

17

*D*arrell heard something rustle in the bushes. He paused, eyes narrowing, checking to see if he saw a nosey woman with dark hair and light gray eyes. Isabeau Rosen was nowhere to be found. Instead, a three-legged cat hobbled past him and up the stairs to the front porch.

The cat turned and stared at him. Then it hissed. The door opened and what could only be described as a model stood in the entry way.

This woman had a lush mane of hair that couldn't decide if it was brown, black, or red. It radiated out in waves from her shoulders. Her skin was pure cream with a hint of almond milk. Her large eyes were hooded by lush, dark lashes. He couldn't pinpoint the color of her irises. They shifted from hazel to green to blue as she cocked her head and stared down at him.

The cat put its tail in the air and wound its way through the woman's long legs. Darrell checked the number on the side of the house to be sure he'd come to the right place.

"Darrell Walker?"

Darrell nodded.

"*Doctor* Darrell Walker?" The woman looked him up and down.

"Leave him alone, Countess."

Darrell heard Duchess' voice coming closer. He'd only had three conversations with the woman. One conversation was under the eager gaze of Beau. The second and third had been between the two of them over the phone. At least he thought it was just the two of them. He had noted some static interference that he wouldn't be shocked to find out was Beau tapping the line.

Beau had badgered him the entire week about his date with Duchess. She queried him about what he would wear, as he adjusted her in his office. Then she'd quiz him on topics of discussion to have on the date while they worked together at the community center in preparation for the Cultural Cotillion. The woman was relentless, and potentially more excited about his date than he was.

Darrell and Duchess were originally meant to go out last weekend, but she'd had to cancel. Beau had nearly had an epileptic fit until Darrell told her that they'd rescheduled. She'd texted him twice today already to be sure that the date was still on.

Duchess appeared in the doorway. Her orange-red hair was piled tamely atop her head. She wore a dress that hugged her ample curves and showed off her shapely legs.

"Hi, Dr. Walker," she addressed the floor as though uncomfortable with his perusal.

Darrell averted his gaze. Behind her, he saw a tall, black boy eyeing him suspiciously.

Duchess reached behind her and brought the kid forward. "This is my son, Tyrone."

The boy couldn't have been more than twelve, but he

had the stature of a man grown. Darrell looked between mother and son. He hadn't figured Duchess anywhere near her thirties. She must have had him while she was still a child herself.

"Mama, mama!"

A toddler flew into the room and wrapped himself around Duchess' legs, causing her to teeter. Darrell's eyes narrowed as he took in the child's jet-black hair and Asian features.

A blond haired boy of about eight or nine trailed behind him and began disentangling the boy. "Sorry, mama. I'll get him back to bed."

Duchess gave the toddler a kiss on the top of his dark head of hair. Then she reached out and kissed the blond boy. She rubbed her hand over the eldest boy's brown cheek. The eldest's eyes were still on Darrell, but he turned and followed the other two brothers out of the room.

Darrell looked between the four of them. Then his eyes landed back on the modelesque sister. Her smile was a challenge; challenging Darrell to run? To make an inquiry?

"You want to go?" Duchess said.

"Yeah, let's." Darrell offered her his arm.

"No," There was a creak in Duchess' voice, like a door opening to allow him the space to get out. "I mean, do you want to go... to bow out... after..." She waved her hand in the general vicinity of her disappearing children.

"That depends?" Darrell said.

Beside Duchess, her sister took what could only be described as a fighting stance.

"I'll go," he said, "if you're coming with me." Darrell smiled and offered his arm again.

Duchess blinked. Her fingers trembled as she reached for and took his arm.

Countess stepped in front of them, blocking the door. "What's the name of the restaurant you're going to?"

"Thanks for sitting the kids, Tess." Duchess shoved her sister aside and pulled the door open. Once alone on the porch, she faced Darrell. "Sorry about that. My sister's a bit over protective."

As they descended the porch steps to his car, Duchess fidgeted with her dress, pulling at the hem. She looked... different. She'd been in a t-shirt, jeans, and hiking boots at the school. Tonight, she was in a form-fitting dress that showed off her assets very nicely. Her face was brightened with makeup. She looked beautiful, but uncomfortable.

"Your children, too, it would seem," Darrell said. "They're protective, I mean."

She paused as he opened the car door. "Look, if you want to call off the date, just say so."

Darrell straightened from his stooped position of opening the door.

"My kids and I are a package deal," she continued. "I can't always get a babysitter. They can be a handful if unleashed into the world. There are three of them, in case you didn't count. And they're all mine."

The way she said *mine* reminded him of a lioness protecting her cub. Darrell looked down at her cafe au lait colored skin. He knew that albinos could have children who weren't born with the trait. It was clear that none of the children had it. It was also clear that none of the children looked anything like the woman they called mama. It was clear that Duchess claimed each of those boys with her heart, if not her genes. Loyalty was a trait Darrell prized.

He pulled the car door open wide. "I like kids. I volunteer my spare time at the local community center."

"You do?"

"One of the things you'll learn about me if we have dinner together." He indicated the open car door and the empty passenger seat.

Duchess released her firm stance and ducked into the car.

"I was thinking Italian?" he said as he started the car.

"Sounds good. Just know that I'm not a dainty salad eater. I like meat."

Darrell raised his eyebrows.

Duchess blushed, averting her gaze. "I mean animal meat. I'll probably order a steak."

"I like steak, too."

"And sorry, but there's no going dutch. My sister took my credit cards out of my purse. She said if a man is really interested, then he needs to court a woman, and that includes paying for dinner."

"I think I like your sister."

He caught the change of her expression as he turned the corner.

"Everyone does," she said. "She's the pretty one. She got all the looks. I'm just..."

Darrell gave her a side-glance as they neared the restaurant.

"This isn't me." She splayed her hand over the dress.

Darrell shrugged. "I like a woman who's not too fussy with her clothes. I thought you looked very pretty the day I met you."

"Pretty. Not beautiful."

"Outward beauty isn't as important to me as what's on the inside. You love your kids." All three of them. He wondered about their fathers, but he'd wait for that story. "You work with wounded animals."

Duchess was an ER Vet. He'd learned that during one of their brief phone calls.

"Those things are beautiful to me," he continued. "You inspire loyalty from those around you, including your sister. Beau took a liking to you immediately. Be warned; that woman is like the mafia when she decides she's going to be your friend. And don't think you have a say in whether or not you're chosen."

"You and Beau are close?"

"We're..." Darrell hesitated as he thought about his relationship with Beau, if he could call it that. He barely knew the woman. Yet, he did know her. He knew that she wore her heart on her sleeve. He knew that she was a romantic. He knew that she wanted people to be happy. She saw the world through rose-colored glasses, completely ignoring the fog. "We're friends."

"You don't sound certain."

"Because I didn't have a choice in the matter. She just sort of adopted me."

"Yeah, people who adopt others are cool."

Darrell wondered if that was the story of her three sons. But Duchess let the silence reign on. He decided to change the subject. Unfortunately, he couldn't remember any of Beau's approved topics.

"My mother lives in a retirement community in Florida and my dad skipped out on us when I was young," he said. Then he winced. "Is this too heavy for first date conversation?"

"No, it's fine," she said. "You haven't heard my crazy yet. Not that I'm crazy. I just have some baggage."

"Everyone has baggage."

They didn't unload their baggage at dinner. As per Gage's advice, Darrell followed the protocol that first dates were like a job interview. And so he only talked about his best traits. Though the dating app hadn't worked out for Darrell, he had found that advice was sound.

Darrell told Duchess about his work at the community center. Duchess told him about her passion for animal rights and her work with wounded and abused animals. They stuck to their service work, and before he knew it, the check came.

"I'm not very good at dating," she said as they walked up to her house at the end of the evening.

"Me, neither. But I really enjoyed myself tonight."

Duchess was everything he was looking for. She was loyal, kind, and smart. He gazed down into her green eyes, preparing to interpret any signs. Before he came across any signals, his phone beeped.

He chuckled as he looked down at the screen. "Right on cue."

He showed Duchess the name on the screen. She didn't chuckle in return as she read Beau's name and the text beneath it.

"She seems very invested in the outcome of our date," Duchess said.

"Well, she thinks she's a matchmaker."

"Yeah, she said that; that she saw us together in a dream."

"You're not from around here, are you? You don't know about the Charmaynes."

"No, I'm from around here. I know all about the Charmayne's and their magic."

Duchess' tone was sweet, but with a bitter center. Darrell did not want to investigate that rabbit hole. They'd had a great night and he wanted it to end that way.

"I'd like to see you again," he said.

"Okay." Duchess took a deep breath, and then let it out in a gush. "I'd like that too."

"Are you sure?"

She took another breath, but this one she let out slowly and quietly. "I've been very unlucky in the love department. I'm a little gun-shy."

"I've been unlucky, too. Maybe our luck is about to change?"

They stared at each other. Darrell was hesitant to lean in. He hadn't gotten this far with a woman in a while. But Beau had told him that this woman was his dream girl, his One.

He decided to take that as his sign and leaned in.

Duchess leaned in too.

Their lips met. Her lips were soft and warm. She sighed again and the gust of air met the top of his lip.

She pulled back first. "Thanks, Darrell."

"Thank you, Duchess."

"My friends call me Ducky."

Darrell smiled. "Good night, Ducky."

She ascended the steps and waved over her shoulder before disappearing inside.

Darrell stood on the bottom stair of the porch. He touched his fingers to his lips. Duchess was everything he could have asked for. They spoke the same language. They both were a bit awkward, awkward enough so that neither of them felt uncomfortable. He could talk shop with her. He felt comfortable around her.

It didn't matter one bit that there hadn't been a spark in that kiss.

18

"Why do we have to go out tonight?"

Beau looked over at her husband. His pout was so much like his son's that she had to blink a couple of times to bring him into focus. Philip was dressed in a dark, gray suit. Or was that actually dark blue? She couldn't tell, in the low light of the car's dashboard.

"You said yourself," she said, "now that the callers are taking on a bulk of the work, we have more time to do things together."

Beau still had yet to meet with the consultant, Yohance Stanley. They'd planned for a sit down two days ago, but business had called him out of the country, indefinitely. She had visited his calling center. It was a renovated warehouse with desk upon desk of rotary phones. The Millennials seated in the office chairs looked out of place, with cords dangling down their chests.

This army of dialers could contact more donors in one day than Beau and her small staff could've handled in a month. In just a week, the dialers had amassed the amount of money-donations that Beau had hoped to gain for the quarter. She had to admit it was a good idea. Not only was it a good idea, it was, indeed, allowing her to spend more time at home with her family. This would be the first date night she and Philip had had, that wasn't work related, in... likely since the twins were born.

"My idea of a night out is not having dinner with your stuffy cousin and his ghetto wife," said Philip.

"Mommy what's ghetto mean?"

Beau looked into the rearview mirror and into Flora's inquisitive eyes. Then she glared at her husband, but he had his back to her as he put the car in park and got out. Under the porch lights, his suit revealed itself to be dark blue instead of gray.

She waited for Philip to come around and open her door. Instead, he pulled out his phone and began tapping and swiping. Beau sighed and opened her own car door. Then she went to the rear and released the children from their car seats.

Together they ascended the grand steps. Faun won the race to the top and earned the privilege of ringing the door-bell to the Charmayne mansion. It felt weird, ringing the doorbell, when she had spent so much time here during her youth. But her aunt was no longer the lady of the manor. Pumpkin was.

A young Asian woman answered the door. Beau knew the girl to be one of Pumpkin's former students. They'd met a handful of times before, on the rare occasion that Pumpkin had twisted Beau's arm into a girls' night out.

"Hello, DaeHo."

"Hi, Mrs. Rosen," the young woman beamed. "Hi, Flora. Hi, Faun."

Flora wrapped herself around DaeHo's thin middle. Faun placed his hand in DaeHo's the moment she reached out for him. DaeHo was one of the only people that Faun brightened for. Pumpkin's son, Seth, poked his head out into the hall and ushered the twins and the babysitter into the playroom.

Manny and Pumpkin came down the hall. They were holding hands. She and Philip had had twins within a year into their marriage. They hadn't been holding hands any longer by that time. They weren't holding hands now. Beau took another look at the newest Charmayne newlyweds. It wasn't her imagination that Pumpkin was tugging Manny behind her.

Manny and her brother, Guy, had never taken to Philip. Beau knew it was because they hadn't had the time to get to know him. They'd married quickly, then had the twins, then went into business, which took up all their time. But now that the non-profit was in the hands of the consultant and his callers, they'd have more time to be a family and get to know her family. It was night one in Beau's six-years-late offensive to make her family fall for her husband.

"Manny and I thought we'd try something new tonight," Pumpkin grinned. "How about Ethiopian food?"

"Sounds like fun," Beau said.

"Don't those people eat with their hands?" asked Philip.

Beau and Philip spoke at the same time. Philip's disgruntled voice overtook her chipper one.

"Let's just try it," Beau whispered to him with a strained smile.

She'd spent the day organizing files, writing letters of recommendation for her displaced interns, and making arrangements for the community center's cotillion. Thankfully, Mrs. Paulson and Darrell were helping her on that front.

Actually, the brunt of the work had fallen to Darrell.

Beau felt bad on that front, but Darrell insisted that both the new mother and recently injured mother needed to take it easy. While Beau and Mrs. Paulson plotted over the phone each day, Darrell would take their edict and put it into place at the center. The man was a godsend; for her spine as well as her spirit.

But she still had paper cuts and a headache from trying to rearrange her primary business. She'd had to twist Philip's arm to get him to drive the kids to school, and again to pick them up. He did it, grudgingly, under the stipulation that he use her new car to save the leather interior of his car from the kids' booster seats. She was exhausted now, but she was excited to get out of the house and spend time with other adults.

"So," Manny said, when they sat down and dug, fingers first, into the lentils at the Ethiopian restaurant. "I hear you two are organizing an event for the community center?"

Philip blinked in confusion.

"We are," Beau interjected. "Dr. Paulson..." She looked pointedly at Philip, but the name didn't jar his memory. But then again, he rarely remembered their donors. "Dr. Paulson's wife is the Director at the Community Center. He wanted a way to help refugee children."

"And you thought a fashion show was the way to go?" said Manny.

Guy and Manny teased Beau endlessly. She had great practice in ignoring the good-natured jibbing. "It's a display of the beauty of their cultures and the resilience of their spirit."

Manny cocked his head. "But they'll be in pretty dresses, walking down a runway?"

Beau rolled her eyes, but she couldn't hide her grin. It was so good to hang out with him again.

"So, Philip," Manny turned his attention to her husband. "Business must be great, if your wife is organizing fashion shows."

"Things are well," Philip said. "We hired the nonprofit consultant, Yohance Stanley. He's brought in twenty grand in just the last week."

Beau blinked. She hadn't seen those numbers. She was still unpacking boxes. The accounting files were still a few boxes away.

"Wow, that's amazing," said Pumpkin, as she scooped lentils onto her spongy bread.

"Using professional callers is a revolutionary way to run a nonprofit," said Philip. "You should consider it for Charmayne Charitable Corporation."

Beau saw the skepticism in Manny's jawline. He could chide her, but Philip was a little bit more sensitive. She jumped in before dinner turned into an argument. "Plus, we're able to spend more time with our family. So, it works for everyone."

Philip's phone rang. Beau, Manny, and Pumpkin had all turned their phones off when they sat down. "Excuse me, I have to take this."

"Be careful about this, Beau," said Manny, after Philip walked away from the table. "Short cuts usually cost more than you expect."

"You've never liked him." Beau shook her head as she dragged her spongy bread through the orange, spicy lentils.

"It's not that I don't like him. I just don't know him very well."

"He's my One, Manny."

"Yeah, you can't help that." Manny wrapped an arm around his wife and stared into her eyes as though Beau wasn't there.

The love between them was palpable. Beau looked out the window and saw Philip laughing into his phone. Their eyes caught. She looked into his blue eyes and smiled. He blinked and turned away.

"Did you find out how Darrell's date went?" Pumpkin asked.

Beau turned back to her friend, thankful for the change of topic.

"How do you know Darrell?" Manny asked.

"The car accident," answered Pumpkin. "She went to him for an adjustment."

"Darrell's dating again?" asked Manny.

"Beau saw his dream girl in a vision."

Manny turned to Beau, finally including her in the conversation. "You're seeing visions again? When did this happen?"

"After the accident," Beau said. "When Darrell adjusted me for the first time, I fell asleep on his table and I had a vision."

"Of his dream girl?" Manny said. He took his wife's left hand in his, rubbing his thumb over the rock on her fourth finger.

"Uh, no. That wasn't the first thing I saw." Beau looked out the window at her husband. Philip had his back to them and was still on his phone. "But after seeing Darrell a few more times, then I saw her. Her name's Duchess. They went on a date last week. I haven't had a chance to talk to him about it. I'm seeing him tomorrow."

"I'm glad you saw her," Manny said. "Darrell deserves to be happy."

He brought his wife's hand to his lips for a kiss. Pumpkin smiled adoringly at her husband. Philip paced the sidewalk; his suit turning dark gray in the moonlight, and back to dark blue under the street lamps.

Philip spent most of the dinner on that, and then a second, phone call. But dinner was not a bust. Manny regaled her with tales of tackling city issues as the new mayor. They also caught up on family gossip. It made Beau realize how much she'd missed spending time with her extended family.

When they got home, Philip shut himself into the office to take some more phone calls. Beau tucked the kids into bed. They went immediately to sleep after their evening with DaeHo and Seth. Beau got under her comforter and made a call.

"Hey, Gee-Gee."

"Oh, Beau-Beau," Guy sighed into the phone. "I think I'm in love."

Those were the last words she expected to hear from her playboy brother.

"With your artist, Agave?"

"No, her name's Midori."

"Midori? Midori Miller? The woman who made Pumpkin's wedding dress?"

"She's changed me, healed me, Beau-Beau. I feel like a new man."

Guy went on to tell Beau about his lackluster attempts to stay away from the dressmaker and how he'd failed miserably. Beau had met the woman a few times while Pumpkin was on fittings. She'd come to like the woman in those few encounters. She was excited to get even closer to her new sister-to-be, after hearing Guy's stories of their mishaps and adventures in New York City.

"How are things between you and Philip?"

"Things are great." Even she didn't believe the falsetto of

her voice.

Her brother didn't fill the silence, but he also didn't challenge her.

"Things are just a little stressful after the accident," she said. "And things are changing in the business. I envy you at the start of your romance. I miss that stage."

"Well, you two did get married rather quickly," Guy said.

"There was no reason to wait when we knew it was true love." There was another tense silence after the defensiveness in her voice.

They'd had this argument time and time again. When Beau first brought Philip home, Guy was not convinced.

"Are you sure it's true love or just a positive pregnancy test?" he'd so tactfully asked.

Beau hadn't spoken to her brother for weeks after that. Not until her wedding day. He'd never made another disparaging remark about the love of her life since. But neither did he say anything positive.

"Yeah, I get it now," Guy said. "You see the world differently when you're happy and in love."

If that were true, then why was Beau's world turning upside down now?

She knew that Manny wasn't able to see gold until he met Pumpkin. Guy, who'd been able to spot talent by looking at a person, had lost his Sight for a while. Now that he'd found Midori, he was healed and seeing clearly again. It was the opposite with Beau. When she'd met Philip, her magic left her.

It hadn't come back ...until she met Darrell.

Beau got off the phone with her brother. She was tired, but she knew it would take her a while to fall asleep, if she fell asleep at all. The moment she put her head to the pillow, she was out like a light.

When she opened her eyes, she was in the garden but she wasn't alone. Darrell was beside her. He smiled at her and then turned to Duchess.

Darrell let go of the small of Beau's back and joined Duchess at her side. Beau watched the two walk off together, past her, smiling and laughing. Darrell put his hand on Duchess' lower back. An ache settled in Beau's gut.

She turned to the cliff. Philip stood there facing her. He looked as though he was waiting for her to come to him.

Beau took a step. It was easier now to move forward. She made her way to the overlook. As she got closer and closer, she was able to see what was down below the cliff. A boat.

The faces were familiar on the boat. She saw her aunt Gale. She saw Manny and Pumpkin. She saw her brother, and beside him she saw Midori Miller. She saw her three cousins, Christian, Isla and Judas, and a various assortment of other faces. There was even DaeHo and the blond-haired boy she called her boyfriend.

They all waved her towards them. Beau took a step. But something called to her and she turned around.

Philip stood a few steps away from her. Behind him, storm clouds were moving in. They looked ominous.

Philip stared at the clouds, transfixed. Beau called to him, he didn't answer. She reached out to him and got a handful of his blue suit. She tugged at him, but he didn't budge.

A sense of urgency lit a fire under her feet. The clouds were nearly upon them. She had to do something. She had to save him.

She put her hand against his heart. It was the first time she'd ever touched him in the dream. He blinked and looked down at her... like he didn't know her.

And then she woke up.

19

She was the first thing Darrell saw when he entered his office. Her dark hair was down around her shoulders today. She wore a bright blouse and dark jeans. He paused in the doorway, realizing how excited he was to see her. Then he paused to try and figure out why he was so excited to see her.

She'd been a thorn in his side for these past couple of weeks.

No, not really. She hadn't been a thorn; at least not a painful one.

She'd poked and prodded him towards his goals of finding a partner. She'd been on his side, pushing him and cheering for his happiness. Thanks to her, he'd found a partner who met his needs.

Darrell moved towards Beau as though there was a magnet pulling him to her. She didn't look up at him. Her gaze was trained out the window.

Outside, there were storm clouds on the horizon. Worry creased Beau's brow. There was heaviness in her light eyes.

Darrell balled his fists instead of reaching out to her.

She had no qualms about touching him, but it would be highly improper, not to mention unprofessional, for him to be so familiar with her outside of corrective measures to her spine.

"Mrs. Rosen," he called. But she didn't budge or break contact with the clouds out the window. "Beau?"

She turned at the sound of her given name. The worried crease lifted a fraction as she regarded him. A small smile played at her lips.

"Darrell," she sighed.

Darrell had the urge to fall into the seat next to her, take her into his arms, and hold her tightly to him. He didn't like the heaviness that surrounded her. He didn't like that something creased her perfect brow. It bothered him that her lips faced the wrong direction.

But he didn't fall into the chair. He knew how to relieve the heaviness from her. He reached out a hand to her and she took it.

His palm tingled where the pads of her fingers met his. The energy went up his wrist, through his forearm, and into his chest. That wasn't static cling or shock. He had no scientific explanation for it.

He looked down at her. The crease of worry was gone from her forehead. Her eyes were open wide. Her light eyes had lost their darkness. He noted there were no bags under her eyes.

"You've been sleeping?"

"Hmm? Oh, yes." She withdrew her hand and looked away from him. "I've been sleeping well, thank you."

"Any new dreams?"

She tugged her lip into her mouth, looking uncomfortable.

"Why don't we get you on the table?" He preceded her to

the exam room, then turned and held the door open for her. She nearly collided with him. But he caught and steadied her back onto her feet.

And there it was again; electricity sizzling through his skin at the places where he contacted hers. Her eyes went wide, almost fearful.

Darrell didn't like her looking at him with anything but a smile. He let her go and backed away so that she could enter the exam room without touching him again.

Once inside, he remembered what he was there to do. He would be touching her skin directly. Moving the bones and tendons to offer her relief.

She lay down on the table, face down. She closed her eyes and sighed. He began his palpations, but the tension he sensed was not in her back.

"Beau? Is everything okay?"

"I... I just had a strange dream last night. I don't know what to make of it."

"Do you want to talk about it?" He released her spine and pulled up a rolling chair to sit before her.

She sat up on the exam table, her feet dangling like a little girl's. "Oh, I don't want to bother you with my problems. I've intruded enough into your life as it is."

"We're friends, right?"

She smiled then, a real, undistracted smile aimed right at him.

She nodded. She took a deep breath and raised her light gray gaze to meet his. Those eyes reminded him so much of his old friend's that it caught Darrell's breath. For the first time in nearly a year, he wondered how Manny was doing?

"I'd rather hear about your date," Beau said.

Darrell refocused on the Charmayne before him. He felt

a moment's disappointment that she didn't confide her worries in him.

"I'm supposed to get details to bring back to Manny and Pumpkin," she said.

"Manny and Pumpkin?"

"They wanted word about you. They want you to be happy. We all want you to be happy."

"Why?"

"You're part of the family."

She said this as though it were crystal clear, as though she'd known him all his life.

"Manny knows you're still mad at him," she continued. "But he misses you. He wants you to find love because..." She gave a little chuckle. "You see the world differently when you're happy and in love."

As she said the words the storm clouds moved back into her gray eyes and the crease returned.

"Are you happy, Beau?" He had no clue why he asked it.

No, that wasn't true. He did know. He'd seen it the first day she'd walked into his office. The smile she'd worn then was practiced and plastic, just as it was now as she prepared to lie to him. The smile a second ago, when he'd confirmed their friendship... that smile was the real Beau.

"Of course I'm happy," she said.

The plastic smile shivered. Darrell saw it splinter on the right side of her face. But he knew she needed to hold onto it, and so he let her.

"Face down, please." He indicated the exam table.

Her eyes thanked him and then her body complied with his edict.

Darrell stood slowly, his hands itching. He had to shake them free of their eagerness. This was business. She couldn't be his friend right now. She was his client and he would tend to her wounds, only the external ones that he could reach. It wasn't his place to reach inside and touch the internal hurts.

"The kids are doing well?" He rolled up the hem of her shirt to expose her curved back.

"Faun has a crush on the babysitter. And Flora is still waiting for her date with you." Her voice was light as she talked about her children.

Darrell placed his thumbs at the base of her spine. They both inhaled at the impact. Darrell swallowed and began to manipulate the tissue around her spine. She had healed up marvelously.

"You can start driving again," he said.

"Hmmm?" was her only response.

"And you can go back to work as early as tomorrow."

"Philip brought the office home, so I'm already kinda back at work. Filing papers and making calls; nothing strenuous."

He watched the tension in her back. His fingers traced it. His thumb chased and he pushed it away. She sighed.

When he was finished, she sat up and straightened her shirt. "What day should I schedule our next appointment?"

There really wasn't much more he could do for her. Her spine was holding firm. "You're as good as new, Beau."

She smiled at that, the genuine smile.

"You don't need my services anymore."

The smile melted away. "Don't I need maintenance or wellness check-ups or... something?"

"Once or twice a month is normal wellness care for spinal health."

"You trying to get rid of me, Dr. Darrell?"

"No." Darrell said the word a little more vehemently

than he'd meant. "Your body has healed itself. I just helped it along."

"You helped me a lot. Healing from the accident and helping me to get my visions back. And all of your help with the cotillion."

"Just because you're well, it doesn't mean we don't get to see each other outside of the office. Maybe a double date?"

Something that Darrell couldn't name crossed her features. "That would be fun," she said with the plastic smile. Another crack appeared on the other side of her mouth.

Darrell helped her down from the exam table. They walked to the door silently. The energy buzzing between them was like an army of bees in his ears. Beau turned and he nearly crashed into her this time, but he was able to halt before falling into her.

"I'll see you soon?"

To Darrell's ears it sounded like a plea and not a question.

"Very soon," he soothed. "At the Cultural Cotillion. I still have a date with your daughter."

Her eyes brightened. "She's a lucky girl. She and Duchess"

He nodded. They lingered a moment. And then she turned and left. Darrell's fingers still tingled.

20

"Faunie, can you help me?"

Beau watched Flora as she struggled to tie her hair bow. When Beau began teaching the twins to tie their own shoes, Faun exceeded where Flora lagged behind. It was something he liked to remind his sister of every time they sat at the front door and he laced up his sneakers while she slipped on a pair of ballet flats.

Faun took one look at the lacy bow, crossed his arms, and frowned at her. "I'm not tying a bow in your hair. That's girl stuff."

Beau pinched her lips together before she prepared to interrupt. She wanted to raise a gentleman of a son, not a chauvinist who believed in the separation of the sexes.

"Beau," Philip called from down the hall.

She sighed and turned down the hall leaving the twins to their own devices. A twinge rang in her lower back as she did so. That had been happening more and more since she'd been working from home with her husband. She wondered if Darrell had released her from his care too soon. The thought of the good doctor's hands pressing and molding her back into health was a welcome one as she walked down the hall to her husband.

"Beau, where are the videos of the food drive we did last year?" Philip stood in the midst of a mess of paperwork. Paperwork she'd spent the last two days organizing.

She ran the sentence back in her head: *Food drive we did?* She couldn't remember Philip working on a food—Oh! He must mean the food drive she'd organized with a local church group. It had happened on a beautiful, sunny day in the fall. Philip had gone off for a round of golf, promising to catch her up. He never showed.

She looked around the piles of boxes. "I'm not sure? I didn't pack these boxes."

"Babe, I need those videos. Stanley wants to reedit the footage. He says there's a lot of money to be raised when people think kids are starving and dying of thirst."

"But those kids weren't starving or dying of thirst. It was a food drive for Thanksgiving in the parish."

Philip brushed the fact away. "He told me that a million dollars was raised in the name of kids with polluted waters."

"The kids of Saint Anne's aren't drinking polluted waters."

"But many of the rivers in Louisiana are polluted. The rest is semantics."

"Philip, the Rosen Foundation doesn't tell bold-faced lies to get money."

"About that, Stanley says we should consider an offshoot arm for this venture. Call it the Charming Fund."

"But people might confuse it with the Charmayne Fund."

"Exactly." Philip twirled his index finger in the air. "I can't believe I didn't think of that myself. It's brilliant marketing. We could get some of the Charmayne donors without any of the work. I just need you to find those videos. I can't believe you haven't gotten around to all of these boxes yet. Didn't that doctor clear you to get back to work?"

"He did." Beau reached behind and pressed the heel of her hand into the ache at her low back. "Closing the physical office hasn't taken anything off my plate. It's added more. It's just you and me now, and I really need help."

Philip sighed heavily, as though she'd laid down a great burden on him. "We're supposed to be partners, Beau."

She had to unclench her jaw to force the words out. "Partnership doesn't mean that I do everything."

"What's that supposed to mean?" Philip fixed his stare on her. "I'm trying to make this company profitable, and you're..."

"What?" She crossed her arms over her chest. "I'm what?"

He took a step back. "You're the one taking time off and leaving me to pick up the pieces."

Pieces? What pieces? If anything, he'd smashed the solid foundation their business had sat upon and handed her a million, jagged shards that she had to put back together.

"I was in a car crash." She shut her eyes and spoke slowly, trying to temper the white, hot flashes of anger fogging her gaze. "But somehow, I'm still doing my job, in addition to the work you've added on top of it, plus taking care of the kids like always, and doing all of the housework. How exactly is that a partnership, Philip?"

He threw his hands up. "I'm trying to make this work, Beau. I'm trying to make *us* work."

Beau opened her eyes. The lighting in the room was dim, but she saw him clearly.

Philip sat at the edge of the desk. He hung his head looking defeated. "Sometimes, I feel like you don't even see me."

She went to him, taking his hands in hers. His palms were clammy and cold. "What are you talking about?"

"I never wanted to run a nonprofit. I did it for you. I didn't want kids, but I did the right thing when you got pregnant."

The room started spinning. What was he saying? Beau squeezed his hands, seeking his strength. But his hands were limp in hers.

"I keep trying and trying," he continued. "Sometimes I wonder what the hell I'm doing all of this for? We're both unhappy."

Beau shook her head vehemently. "I'm not unhappy."

He raised an eyebrow at her.

She came closer to him, settling herself between his thighs and placing her hands on his shoulders.

Philip placed his hand at her low back. A dull ache settled there instead of relief.

"We're just going through a rough patch," she said. "Everything's going to be fine after..."

After what? He'd said everything would be fine after the kids were born. And then once the business got off the ground. And now? What was left? They were living 'the after.' Why wasn't it happy?

Philip studied her face. "Why do you fight so hard for this, for us?"

"Because, you're..." But the words froze on her tongue. He was her dream man. He'd turned around in her dream and she'd seen his face. But there had been storm clouds in her dream garden.

"I remember when we met you said you saw me in a

dream," Philip said. "You said I was standing in a garden. You based one of the biggest decisions of your life on that hunch. Why don't you trust me in my decisions in real life?"

She opened her mouth to say, 'I do.' But the words stuck in her throat.

"This thing with Yohance Stanley and the business, I've thought this through. I have actionable evidence."

He reminded Beau of Darrell just then. Darrell insisted on proof and facts for a non-quantifiable phenomenon such as love. Here, her husband had stats to prove a business tactic. Beau shuffled her feet, causing her body to sway. She glanced down as Philip unwound his fingers from hers.

"Will you find those videos for me please?"

Beau nodded, not meeting his eye.

"I'm headed out for a meeting."

"But it's Saturday. We have the event at the Community Center tonight."

Philip frowned. "What does that have to do with me?"

"It's the Cultural Cotillion event we're putting on. You're supposed to walk Flora down the stage."

"Beau, I don't have time to play around. We're running a business here. Just take her to a playground or get her a new doll. She'll be fine. She won't even remember this in a few years."

Beau watched her husband leave through the office door. Then she heard Flora ask him for help with her hair bow.

"Ask your mom," was his reply.

And then she heard the front door shut behind him..

She turned back to look at the files and boxes. The tension in her neck returned. There was heaviness in her limbs.

Beau reached for her cell phone. The recent calls

showed her brother, Pumpkin, and Darrell. Beau skipped over her relatives' names.

"You're a menace, you know that?"

"I am?" Beau's heart thumped at Darrell's words, but she noted the chuckle at the end of his statement.

"I told you I'd tell you about my date with Duchess when I see you later tonight at the cotillion."

"Oh. Right. Your date."

"That is why you're calling, right?"

It wasn't why she was calling. She had no idea why she'd clicked on Darrell's number instead of one of her family members. Darrell didn't like Philip any more than the rest of her family.

"Or are you worried over some last minute detail about tonight's event?" he asked. "I told you, we've got everything under control."

The ache that had been in her back dulled to near non-existence with just his words. Beau couldn't put any words of her own together. She could only sigh.

"How are you feeling this morning, Beau?"

Darrell's question took her aback. His voice was bright and chipper, friendly, soothing. The truth was on the tip of her tongue, but instead she said. "I'm doing fine, Dr. Darrell. Just fine."

"I'm glad to hear my services have paid off. You sleep well?"

She hadn't slept well last night. She hadn't slept through the night. She'd woken up a number of times. "I slept okay."

"But no dreams? You calling to get another appointment with the magic hands?" he chuckled.

The idea of Darrell's table and his hands on her spine was a welcome one, but she couldn't keep using him as a crutch.

"Beau?" His laughter stopped, and concern laced his voice. "Is something wrong?"

Something was wrong, but she wasn't sure exactly what it was. No, that wasn't true. She wasn't ready to face exactly what it was. She was running to the closest thing that had given her comfort. Once upon a time, that would have been her brother. But Guy was in bliss with his new girlfriend and he'd be all too happy to point out everything he believed Philip had done wrong in their marriage. And Beau suspected Guy's list would be long.

"Beau, is this something you can't talk to your husband about?"

Her hesitation must have lasted a second too long.

"Is this something *about* your husband?"

"No," Beau lied. "I was just calling because... Flora might not be able to make it tonight."

"Oh, no, she was looking forward to it."

"Yeah, she was. But something's come up."

"She's a five-year-old little girl. What could've come up in her schedule?"

The silence between them spoke volumes.

"You know, Beau, if business is calling her father away, I could be her chaperone. I don't mind."

Tears welled in Beau's eyes. "You'd do that for her?"

"Of course. She promised me a date. I have a reputation to protect. I can't get stood up by a five-year-old."

Beau giggled like a little girl, and then she hiccupped a cry.

"Will you do something for me?" he said. "Take it easy today. Make a cup of tea and just rest. Even though I cleared you, I don't want you going full speed ahead. Ease your way back into your normal life."

Beau let his care wash over her. Did she want to ease her

way back into her normal life? Was she even sure anymore what her normal life was?

"Thanks, Darrell. You take such good care of me."

"I'd be a crappy friend, otherwise. Listen, I gotta go. I'm headed out to pick up Duchess."

Beau jerked like someone had slapped her face. "I'm so sorry. I didn't mean to keep you."

"You didn't. We're going out for lunch. Then I'll head over to the center and make sure everything is in order for tonight."

"You don't have to do that. It's my responsibility."

"That's not how we do it at the community center. We all work together."

Beau was silent. These last few years, she'd grown used to taking on everything by herself. But it hadn't always been like that. Her family rallied around each other. Philip hadn't grown up like that. She'd thought she could teach him, but it hadn't quite worked out that way.

"Take care of yourself," Darrell insisted, "and I'll see you tonight, okay?"

"Yes, okay."

"Good bye, Beau."

"Goodbye, Darrell. Have fun on your date."

21

———

*D*arrell sat at Duchess' kitchen table. The breakfast dishes were still out. Spilled milk pooled on the plastic tablecloth. He heard her speaking calmly to her youngest son from upstairs while the child wailed his disagreement.

Darrell rose from his seat. He pulled the dishes from the sink and placed them in the dishwasher. He rung out the dish rag and wiped the table down.

By the time he straightened, Duchess framed the kitchen entrance. "You don't have to do that."

Darrell shook his head with a chuckle. He didn't understand the idea of not doing what he saw needed to be done. "It's no big deal." He tossed the rag into the sink. "Is your sister able to make it?"

Duchess shook her head. "I know I've canceled on you two nights in a row. I thought lunch would be a sure thing, but my youngest got sent home from school today."

"Do you want to take him with us? It could be a treat."

"He doesn't do too well in restaurants. As you can hear, he doesn't exactly use an indoor voice."

The boy sang at the top of his lungs. It wasn't an angry shout. The child sounded happy. Darrell knew that some children with Autism did this to self soothe. Duchess hadn't confirmed the health status of her child, but Darrell's degree afforded him some knowledge on the matter.

"He had a bad day," his mother said. "The teachers couldn't control him and they called me to come and get him. This, unfortunately, happens a lot. Makes dating hard."

"Do you want to order in?" Darrell asked. "Or we could make something?"

"You don't want to leave?" Duchess frowned at him. "I was surprised to see you were still here when I came down."

"You know you're not scaring me," he said. "I've dated single mothers before." Though it hadn't worked out with Pumpkin, he still had a great relationship with her son.

"My kids aren't the average. Two of my boys have Autism. And my oldest has been labeled ADHD. It's never a dull moment here. It's also not very sexy."

Darrell shrugged. "I was awkward growing up."

Duchess scratched her temple. "I can't figure you out? You can see that I'm not rich." She waved her hands around her functional kitchen with mixed-matched furniture. "I'm not some great catch." She flung her hands up and down her body. "Why are you still here? And don't tell me that it's because we're compatible. How often do people get together because they're compatible? One person is usually reaching higher."

"Beau saw us in a dream. She said we were fated."

"And that's the only reason you asked me out? Because Beau Rumpel told you she saw us together in a dream?"

"It sounds ridiculous when you say it like that," Darrell

scratched his chin. "But she's relentless. She's determined to match me up. She says I deserve my happy ending."

"I get it now." Duchess nodded slowly. "You're into Isabeau Rumpel, aren't you?"

"What?" Darrell focused on Duchess. "No, and her name's Rosen now. She's married."

Duchess held up her hands. "You don't have to explain. Of course you're into her. She was the most popular girl in high school. Everyone was into her."

"I didn't go to school with Beau."

Duchess went to the cabinet and pulled out a bowl. She reached to the top of the refrigerator and pulled out a bag of fruit.

"She's married," Darrell repeated.

"She's beautiful." Duchess picked out grapes and apple slices and put them into the small bowl.

"You're beautiful," Darrell insisted.

Duchess shook her head. "I can't believe this is happening to me. Again."

"Duchess, I don't know what you're talking about."

"Why am I always second best?" She shoved the fruit back into the fridge and slammed the door.

"I'm here with you."

She rounded on him. "I know I'm not super model beautiful like Beau or my sister. I don't pretend to be. I'm smart. I'm good to animals. I'm loyal to the people I care about."

That was Darrell's entire list. Why did those key elements sound so trivial coming from her lips? "Those are all great qualities," he said.

"Yeah, I know." Her eyes softened. "I see them in you, too. But if I decide to get into a relationship, I don't want to be someone's second choice. I want to be their first choice. Their only choice."

Darrell was loath to admit that he understood that. He'd felt second best for most of his life. He wanted to be in someone's spotlight. He wanted to be someone's One.

He leaned back and scrubbed his hand over his face and then to the back of his head. He'd been around the Charmaynes too long, but he knew it was true. He didn't want to spend his whole life unsatisfied. He wanted to glow for someone like Pumpkin did for Manny. He wanted to see someone in his dreams like Beau had done with her husband.

He looked up at Duchess, this woman who met all of his specifications. He could try to woo Duchess. He could make a life with her. Couldn't he?

"Duchess, you are an amazing woman. I haven't known you long, but I think you're selling yourself short."

"I am short," Duchess said.

"I'm tall," he said.

"My skin is splotchy and my hair is orange."

"My feet point out and, when I walk, I look like a duck."

She snorted a laugh. "We're a mess."

Darrell laughed, and nodded in confirmation.

"But just because we're both a mess doesn't mean we should settle for each other," she said, "and not the person we truly want."

"I'm not in love with Beau Rosen."

He wasn't.

Though truthfully, Isabeau Rosen checked every tick on his list too. She was kind and smart and loyal; loyal to another person despite a number of indications that her husband didn't deserve her devotion. Beyond his list, every time they touched he felt something. He had tried to ignore it. But every time he touched her it was evident in the tingle of his skin.

That didn't mean he was in love with her. He wasn't. He could admit that he liked having her around. As a friend. Just like he liked Duchess.

"I've been burned before, Duchess. It sounds like we both have. Wouldn't it be smarter to have a relationship based on mutual respect and compatibility? Affection can grow from that. I like you. We get along. Shouldn't that be enough?"

She didn't answer at first. And then, "I don't want to get my hopes up. I have three children with special needs. And there are other things in my past that are a lot for someone to deal with."

"Do I look scared?" He gave her a mock face that caused her to giggle.

"You're a really decent guy, Dr. Darrell Walker. I didn't think there were any left. I'd be a fool to let you go, wouldn't I?"

Darrell leaned forward and Duchess met him in the middle. As their embrace closed in, a spark of electricity zapped them apart. The spark was a static one between her sweater and his shirt.

22

*B*eau entered the community center expecting chaos. What she found was everything running in an orderly fashion under Darrell's command. Darrell stood calmly at the center, fielding questions, directing people, shooing Mrs. Paulson, with her squirming baby in her arms, back into a comfortable chair.

Flora and Faun let go of their mother's hand and raced around the gym oohing and ahhing. Beau stood still and did the same. A different culture was represented in every corner of the center's gym.

There were multicolored beads of red, green, and yellow draped over cloth of the same color. A sign above the display proudly proclaimed the country of Sudan.

In another corner, intricate streamers hung from the ceiling over a sign for Bolivia. They were the same colors represented in the display, but thrown into the mix of reds, greens, and yellows were pastel purples and blues.

In each corner of the gym, Beau saw a banner of ownership above an explosion of color. In the center of the room was a raised platform for a stage and folding chairs fanning out to the back of the gym where she stood. She couldn't believe they'd pulled this off in just two weeks.

Darrell turned to her just then. Their eyes locked. Electricity sizzled in the air. He took one step and then another towards her. She watched the play of muscles beneath his crisp white shirt. She hadn't noticed the broadness of his chest before. She had the urge to go to him, to place her hand in his, and lean into the strength of him.

He made his way to her, but before he reached her a little ball of crinoline slammed into him.

"Mr. Darrell are you ready for our date?" Flora spun around in a fluff of gauzy white.

"I sure am, sweetheart." Darrell reached over and grabbed a gray jacket. He slipped it on his broad shoulders. Beau lost her breath as Darrell turned around, beaming at her daughter. He looked exactly like the man in the dream she'd had years ago. Exactly.

She'd never told Darrell the extent of her dream. But here he was, standing before her looking like he'd stepped out of her dreams. Beau couldn't breathe. She couldn't speak.

"I just have a few more things to take care of, okay?" he said to Flora. "Why don't you see if anyone needs help with their decorations? I heard you are quite the artist."

Flora preened under his compliments. She took off in a happy fluff.

"Hey," Darrell said to Beau.

It took a moment for her voice to find itself. She couldn't speak until she blinked and tore her eyes away from Darrell's broad shoulders in that gray jacket. Beau turned to face the wall of decorations instead of looking directly at him.

"I can't believe you did all this," she said.

"I didn't. The community did. The children made the decorations during the afterschool program. Their families brought the flags of their countries. I've just been standing here and pointing to where things should go."

Beau shook her head in disbelief. Organizing an event had never been this simple for her. Well, it had been when she was younger and worked for her family's charity. Back then her cousins, aunts, and uncles had all been there to lend a hand. She missed those times. It had never felt like work. It always felt like a holiday gathering or the Sunday night dinners they'd have at Charmayne House.

"Everything is pretty much in order," Darrell said.

Beau blinked. "Really? You don't need me to do anything?"

"Well, no." He looked around the hustle and bustle of the room, rubbing his thumb across his strong chin. "You left detailed instructions which I followed. There were some things I wasn't sure about, so I waited until you got here so we could discuss them."

Beau couldn't help but cringe at the W word. The last man she left in control had ripped order apart and shoved it back at her to put together. The thought of going back home to her office brought forth a low, wail of pain in the middle of her back. She reached for her low spine and pressed her knuckles into the groove.

Darrell reached for her hip. "What's going on back there?" The moment his fingers grazed her side the electricity snap, crackled, and popped between them.

He should've pulled away from her, but he didn't. She should've pulled away from him, but she didn't. Instead, he stepped closer. He placed his forefinger under her chin and tilted her head up. Beau swallowed. He had been closer to her than this, but this felt different.

"You feeling okay?" He looked directly into her eyes. Well, not into her eyes. He looked at the bags under them. "I thought we'd fixed that insomnia problem. Have you been getting enough rest?" Darrell peered at her over his glasses, with his doctor's expression.

Warmth flooded through Beau from the look. The crick evaporated. The weariness that had plagued her all day disintegrated and she felt ready to take on the world, but Darrell had left her with nothing to do. She didn't know what to do with herself without a long list of to-do's.

"Did I release you too soon? Maybe you need to come in for some maintenance?"

His voice was low, like a lullaby. Beau had the urge to rest her head against his chest.

"You can come in any time," he said. "I'll help you in any way that I can. We're friends, right?"

"I thought I was a pest."

He chuckled. His breath brushed over her, reminding her of the light breeze that lifted the petals in her dream garden.

"A pest?" he said. "I think you would call that a friend. It's been a while since I've had a good friend. Been a while since I've trusted anyone else enough to allow them close enough to become a friend. Thank you for being a pest."

Darrell smiled at her, the genuine, open, friendly smile. She felt caught in that smile. She didn't understand how she'd lived her life without seeing that smile every day. It was like the sun shining its warmth directly on her.

Someone cleared their throat. Darrell looked over Beau's shoulder. Then he jerked away from her.

Beau turned to look behind her.

Duchess stood in the entryway. Her orange-reddish hair was pulled up and slicked back into a stylish chignon. Gone were the jeans, t-shirt, and hiking boots. In its place was a flattering dress that hugged her curves in all the right places. The only thing missing was a bright smile as she came into the arms of the man of her dreams.

Unfortunately, Duchess wasn't able to come into the embrace of the man of her dreams. His arms were otherwise occupied. Darrell dropped his arms and Beau stepped out of them.

"You made it." Darrell approached her and pecked her on the temple.

When he pulled away Duchess stared mutely at him. The tilt of her right eyebrow and the tick in her jaw seemed to Beau like the start of an argument. Or maybe the continuation of one. Before Darrell could open his mouth to cajole, or protest, or respond in anyway, two teens rushed up to him.

"Dr. D," a tall, brown boy huffed. "Carolina is taking over the wall I'm using for America."

"My country is under oppression," Carolina said in a thick accent that reached south of the U.S. borders.

"And you think my people aren't," the boy responded.

"That's enough you two. I'll be over in a second." Darrell turned back to Duchess. "Just let me handle this and I'll be right back."

"No, let me take care of it," said Beau.

"No," Darrell said firmly. "I want you to find a seat and stay there."

"Darrell, I'm fine."

"And you'll stay that way." He turned on his heel and disappeared into the belly of the gym.

Beau turned back to Duchess. The woman's eyebrow was still quirked up in that argumentative way. And now her arms were crossed at her chest.

"I just had a crick in my back," Beau started. "And Darrell has been seeing me —I mean, not seeing me. I've been his patient. He's a wonderful doctor. He healed me. Except, I just had a crick just now, which is why he had his hand on my back."

Beau stopped talking when she noted that her rush of words only made the quirk of Duchess' eyebrow rise higher and higher. After a moment of silence, Duchess narrowed her brows at Beau.

"You don't remember me, do you?" Duchess asked.

Beau concentrated on the woman's face. It was a very unique face. She knew albinism was characterized by a lack of pigment. But to Beau, Duchess' skin looked like rich cream. Under the gym lighting, her hair was golden instead of the orange-red it appeared to be in the sunlight. Her light colored eyes were hypnotic as they shifted from green to blue and back again. Who could forget a face like this?

Before Beau could respond, an unexpected voice sounded from behind her.

"So, I'm here."

Beau turned at the sound of Philip's voice. He looked completely out of place in his light blue suit. "What are you doing here?"

He frowned. "You guilted me into coming."

Beau pulled on her society face at the public accusation. Her society face also doubled as her mom face when Faun threw a tantrum in the grocery store. "I'm so glad you're here," she said. "I want you to meet my friend, Duchess."

Philip turned to Duchess and cringed.

Duchess withdrew her hand. The quirk in her eyebrow turned to steel. "I'm going to go and find a seat."

"That was rude," Beau said to her husband once Duchess was lost in the crowd.

"You didn't tell me this was a charity event for the deformed. You know you have to warn me about things like that so I can put my game face on."

Beau shut her eyes, but her husband's words remained ringing in her ears. There had been other times when Philip had made snide, inappropriate, insensitive comments. She'd shoved those to the back of her mind. But it seemed tonight, they wanted a voice.

She opened her eyes and regarded him anew. "Why are you here, Philip?"

"Had to come." Philip looked around the place with distaste. "There's gonna be local press. Stanley said it would look bad if I wasn't here." Philip smiled as someone with a camera came near. "By the way, we need to find new distributors for some of the items we're donating to needy kids. Stanley thinks we can get them for cheaper and increase our profits."

"Do you mean we or me?"

Philip looked at her quizzically.

"Whenever you say we you usually mean I have to do it."

"What difference does it make? It's for our company. We're a team."

"Are we really? I feel like I do the lion's share, and whenever I ask you for help you don't."

"Where's all of this coming from? Is it because I didn't want to come to this event? You know I don't do well with kids."

"It doesn't matter," she said, the crick in her back returned with a drumstick. "Let's just find some seats."

23

"You look very pretty, Flora."

The little girl preened and twirled under Darrell's admiration.

"She looks like a fart cloud."

Flora stopped twirling and her face fell.

Darrell turned around to see Faun with his arms crossed, looking menacingly at his twin sister. "Faun, that's not a nice thing to say to your sister."

Faun shrugged and made to leave.

"Faun," Darrell put the same bass in his voice that his mother put in hers when he was that age. "Get back here."

The little boy's steps faltered. For a moment Darrell wondered what he would do if Faun didn't heed his words. He knew that if he'd spoken to an elder back in his community in the manner this kid just had, he'd get his butt whooped all the way down the street. Then he'd get whooped again when he got home. This kid wasn't his, nor was he from his old community.

If a kid at the community center took that kind of attitude they'd be given a warning that their attendance at the center was in jeopardy. But again, this kid wasn't a part of the community center. He had no stake in wanting to stay inside where it was safe and off the streets.

From what Darrell could see, Faun was given the reins to ride roughshod over his mother and his sister. He'd obviously learned it from another adult. Darrell had a good idea exactly who that was.

"It's all right, Dr. Darrell," said Flora coming up behind him. "My mommy says he doesn't mean to hurt my feelings when he says mean things."

That was ludicrous. What was the kid's point in saying them then? Darrell didn't believe in the new age quackery of giving kids autonomy to be themselves. They were kids.

"Faun," Darrell spoke quieter but still firmly. The little boy didn't come any closer, but he didn't turn away either. Darrell decided to offer a compromise. He took the few steps necessary to bring him up to the boy. "I want you to turn around and look at me."

Faun did, slowly. His eyes locked down to the ground.

"Faun, that's not how we talk to people we care about."

"I don't care about her." Faun sneered at his sister.

"Yes, I think you do. Otherwise, why would you try to hurt her feelings. Her opinion matters to you."

Faun frowned at Darrell suspiciously.

"Does it make you feel good when you say things to hurt your sister?"

"She's always so annoying."

"Sometimes we want people to look at us and they don't unless we do something wrong. You don't have to do anything wrong to get my attention, Faun. You just need to ask for my attention and I'll give it to you. It's as simple as saying 'hi' to me."

Faun crossed his arms again.

"I'd like to be your friend. But all my friends are nice. They're not mean. If you're my friend we can go and hang out and do things together. Would you like that?"

Faun shrugged, but Darrell saw the dawn of hope in the kid's eyes.

"If we're going to be friends you can call me, Dr. D."

"Can you call me Buck? I don't like my name. People always make fun of it."

Darrell could sympathize. "All right, Buck. You also need to do one more thing for me. Apologize to your sister."

Buck sighed, but he approached his sister. "Sorry, Flora. You don't look like a fart. You look more like snot, which is cool."

"Thank you, Faun," she said with a huge grin. "I mean, Buck."

"Hey, Buck," said Darrell. "How about we both walk your sister out onto the stage for the cotillion?"

Buck looked suspicious again.

"Everyone will get to see you up on the stage," said Darrell.

Buck thought on this and then he reluctantly took his sister's arm, but he did it gently and not with any force.

Darrell peeked out of the curtains and saw Beau seated at the front of the audience. She wasn't alone. Which was good.

He knew the man beside her was her husband. Mainly by the way he looked so out of place. Philip Rosen looked like old money and abundant privilege.

Beau looked like money, but more in a Maid Marion, give to the poor, charitable kind of way. She looked approachable, compassionate, and so beautiful it hurt to look at her.

Darrell blinked. He hadn't meant to think that. He told

those thoughts, those feelings, to hush. They had no business being in his head.

They were likely remnants of his discussion with Duchess earlier. He'd spent most of their time convincing the woman he was interested in dating that he was not pining after Beau. No wonder it was still on his mind.

It hadn't helped that Duchess had walked up on them when he'd been checking Beau out.

Damn, even that phrase sounded proprietary in his mind. But Darrell knew his own thoughts. Beau was his friend. She was his patient. He cared about her well being for both of those reasons. He gritted his jaw at the sight of the tension in her shoulders, as she sat rigidly next to her husband.

There was something wrong there. It annoyed him that she wouldn't tell him what was the matter. Wasn't that what friends did?

Beau looked up and the tension dripped from her jaw. The rigidity seeped from her shoulders. She opened her arms wide, and Manny Charmayne walked into them.

It was the first time Darrell had seen his former friend in months. The huge grin on Manny's face took Darrell aback. He couldn't understand how the man could be smiling. Darrell had spent the last year in lonely, partner-less, buddy-less misery. Manny had broken their friendship and stolen his chance at happiness. He should at least have the decency to look contrite.

But he didn't. He looked happy. He looked a little soft in his midsection, too. A few of the buttons on his shirt tugged.

Good, Darrell sneered from back stage. Mr. Perfect had put on a little weight. The thought thrilled Darrell as he sucked in his firm abs.

Manny gave Beau's husband a stiff nod. All three took

their seats, Beau seated between the two. Her body was turned towards Manny. Mr. Rosen sat stoic while Beau and Manny chatted away like school girls.

From his vantage point back stage, Darrell caught Manny looking around the room every few seconds, as though he was looking for someone. After a few head swivels, Manny froze. He blinked, and stared like a deer in headlights. Then he raised a tentative hand.

Darrell realized Manny was waving at him. Caught off guard, he jerked back until he was hidden behind the curtains.

The program started with a few words from Dr. and Mrs. Paulson. The two brought awareness to the plight raging through Dr. Paulson's ancestral country, as well as the homelands of many of the families present. Then Dr. Paulson turned his praise on Beau and her foundation. He praised the hard work of the children of the community and their families. And finally, the show was underway.

It was nearing Flora's turn on the stage. Darrell took one of Flora's hands while Buck took the other. When they stepped out on stage, she preened like a princess. Buck looked sheepish, but as the applause increased, Darrell saw a smile creep onto the kid's face at the audience's praise and attention.

At the end of the stage, Darrell got a close glance of their mother's face. Her face lit up as she looked at her children. Then she looked up at him. Tears glistened in her eyes. An overwhelming urge to pull her up onto the stage and into his arms came over him.

Out of the corner of his eyes, Darrell glimpsed her husband. The man's smile was plastic. He wasn't looking at his children. His profile was turned to the few press people who were present... and their cameras. Bile rose in Darrell's throat as the threesome turned the edge of the stage and headed back towards the curtains.

Darrell knew what it was like to have an absent father. But it must be worse to have a father in front of you who wasn't truly there. Darrell wanted to jump off the stage and shake the man. Instead, he led the kids off the stage.

Once on the other side of the curtain, Flora bounced up and down and then flew into his arms.

"You did an amazing job, Flora. And you did really good as an escort, Buck."

Buck looked sheepish as he toed at the hardwood floors. Then he was swept up and into his mother's arms as she rushed back stage. She reached out her other arm and swooped Flora up.

"You two were so amazing," she beamed. "You made mommy so proud."

Darrell noticed that Buck looked slightly uncomfortable but he soon relaxed into his mother's embrace.

"Where's daddy?" Flora looked over her mother's shoulder.

Beau's smile faltered. "Um, daddy had to take a phone call. But he saw you and he thought you did really well, too."

Flora lowered her head and picked at a piece of crinoline. Buck hunched his shoulders and kicked a little harder at the wood on the floor. Beau swallowed hard as she looked at her kids.

She looked up at Darrell. Her light gray eyes looked lost. Indecision haunted her features. She took a deep breath and then a step forward. The next thing Darrell knew, she was in his arms.

Darrell gasped as her soft warmth impacted his body. His arms came around her without his permission and then refused to let her go, which was easy because she didn't put up a fight. She stayed in his arms longer than was prudent.

Warmth rushed through Darrell, sparks zapped him everywhere they touched skin to skin. His fingertips were on fire. His cheek sizzled. The place where the air from her nose met his neck was a furnace.

Over Beau's shoulder he caught sight of Duchess. The expression on her face was blank but Darrell read it loud and clear.

"I'm going to treat the kids to ice cream," Beau said. "You should come."

"I can't." He let go of her and stepped out of her reach. "I'm here with Duchess, remember." Darrell looked around, but Duchess was no longer standing back stage.

"Oh, right." Beau's smile turned plastic, professional. "Thank you, Darrell. Tonight was amazing. We'll see you soon?"

Darrell didn't like the way her voice quivered on the question mark. "Of course," he nodded.

After a hug from Flora, and a fist pound from the newly named Buck, the Rosens disappeared into the crowded gym.

Darrell turned and headed in the opposite direction. He knew he was in trouble. His body was alive with the electric shock he'd received from having Beau in his arms. But he had to shut that down. He had to shut it all down. She was not for him.

Darrell moved down the hall, his direction aimless. He just knew he had to put distance between himself and Beau. He wasn't thinking clearly. He wasn't thinking logically.

That hadn't been a look of longing in her eyes. That hadn't been a spark of chemistry between them. There was no chance for the two of them. Beau had seen his dream woman. She'd seen her own dream man. No matter what a douche the guy turned out to be.

God, was he actually calling on dreams to prove common sense? He needed to get an adjustment himself. First on his mind, and then on his spine.

The sound of murmuring brought him farther down the hall. The sound was coming from the coat closet. Darrell sighed as he made his way to the door of the closet. The last thing he wanted to do right now was to break up two teens trying to round the bases.

He knocked. "All right you guys. Button up your clothes and come on out."

Darrell waited.

The door opened and a man stepped out; a grown man. The man had golden-brown skin and light, gray eyes. Darrell stepped back as recognition dawned.

"Hey, Darrell." Manny gave him a tentative smile. "I was thinking of saying 'Fancy meeting you here,' but I'm guessing it's still probably too soon for jokes?"

The last time Darrell and Manny had been in a coat closet, he'd found the man embraced with his girlfriend. But the memory of him and Pumpkin didn't have the same irritable effect that it had had a year ago.

Darrell peered over Manny's shoulder for his wife. Pumpkin's skin looked lighter in the dim lighting of the room. Her dark hair also looked lighter, almost like a reddish-blonde. And then he realized the woman was not Pumpkin Tavares Charmayne.

"You have got to be kidding me," said Darrell.

Manny looked between Duchess and Darrell. "You two know each other?" he asked.

"That's my girlfriend," said Darrell.

Both Manny and Duchess frowned. Manny closed his

eyes and pinched the bridge between his nose. Darrell would have sworn Manny turned a pale shade of green because the man looked like he was about to lose the contents of his stomach.

"This is not what it looks like," Manny insisted. "I'm married." He held up the bright, gold band on his hand as evidence.

"And I'm not your girlfriend," Duchess said. "I think she's married as well."

Darrell opened his mouth to speak. But Duchess walked past him.

"I was grabbing my coat to head home. It was nice seeing you again, Manny." She didn't stomp or storm out. She walked away as though this scene was inevitable.

Darrell let her go, knowing there was nothing he could say to change her mind. It was the truth. He had feelings for another woman, a woman he could never have. A woman who belonged to somebody else.

"I can see that now is not a good time," said Manny. "But when you're ready..." He let the offer hang there.

Darrell actually wanted to talk to Manny. To tell someone what he was feeling. But Manny was the last person he could talk to. What could he possibly say? *I think I'm in love with your married cousin?* Instead, Darrell walked away without a word.

24

"What's the matter, Isabeau my love?"

"I'm fine," Beau said.

Beau turned from her children to look into her aunt's bright, pale gaze. Gale sat beside her in the park while the children played. Flora and Faun —no, Buck. Flora and Buck were getting along quite well this Sunday morning. Beau knew she had Darrell to thank for that. She had Darrell to thank for so much good will in her life right now.

"Then why is it that you're looking so weary?" Gale asked.

This was not the first time Beau or her brother or all of her cousins suspected their aunt's talents ran deeper than just seeing auras.

Gale put a hand to Beau's face. Her thumb went under her eyelid. "The bags under your eyes have cleared. You're finally getting enough rest. But something weighs heavy on your heart. Your aura is more out of balance than usual."

"More than usual?" What did her aunt mean by that? Had she seen her aura out of whack before? If so, she'd never mentioned it.

"I've been telling you that for some time, my dear. It's just now that you seem ready to hear me."

What was with the people in her life telling her they had told her things that she had paid no attention to. First there'd been Philip insisting he made his disdain for gray suits plain to her for years. Had he? And if he didn't prefer gray, like the man in her dreams, did that mean she'd made other mistakes?

"You know, a vow is such an interesting thing," said Gale. "I've always wondered why they called it a solemn promise. Shouldn't it be joyous? You're promising to hold, protect, honor, and cherish someone."

Beau couldn't remember the last time Philip had held her. She felt like she did more of the protection; and that would be protecting him from himself. With the amount of attention he gave to Yohance Stanley, Beau felt that the consultant was more cherished than she was by her husband. The things he was asking her to do with the foundation felt less than honorable.

"A vow is a course of action," Gale continued. "What they don't tell you is that the course can change. And when it does, you may have to make new vows."

Light gray eyes peered into Beau's soul and saw more than she was willing to share. "Philip and I are..."

"Happy? Sweetling, I knew you when you were five, and running through a field of flowers made you happy. I haven't seen you happy in years."

"Why are you telling me this now?"

"Because now I'm beginning to get glimpses of that happy girl again. I'm hoping that whatever is making you happy, you grab onto it. A vow is not a life sentence, Beau. You can change your course."

Change course? Or did she mean change her husband?

Gale had never voiced doubts about Beau's marriage before. Unlike her parents, or her brother, or some of her cousins.

No one had ever said Philip wasn't right for her. That phrase didn't exist in their family; where everyone born with a drop of Charmayne blood would find their one and only true love at some point in their lifetime, and then stay together until the end of their lifespan. There had never been a divorce in the family's recorded history.

The only reason Gale wasn't married was because her fated love had met a tragic end before they could wed. Beau had never once seen or heard Gale express bitterness about it. Whenever her aunt mentioned her paramour it was always with a secret smile and wistfulness in her eyes.

Whenever Beau thought about Philip lately, it was with wariness. Her mind traveled to what fire he'd started that she'd need to put out. Or what new task he'd committed them to that she'd need to squeeze into her already over-crowded schedule. Had Beau ever displayed a secret smile when thinking of her husband? Had her eyes ever been wistful at the thought of him?

"I think having an adjustment has turned your life around," said Gale. "Maybe I'll make an appointment to see Dr. Darrell soon."

Beau smiled at the mention of Darrell's name. Her eyes went far away as she thought about how he'd brought her children together last night. She remembered the strength and security and peace of being in his arms.

"Yes, I think I definitely will make an appointment with the good doctor." Gale looked at Beau slyly.

Beau's shoulders jutted back. "There's nothing going on between me and Darrell. He's just a friend."

"I didn't say otherwise." Gale nodded her head thoughtfully.

Beau opened her mouth to launch a protest, but her attention was diverted as three new children ran onto the playground. They brought Beau's mind back to last night's Cultural Cotillion. The oldest boy was brown. The one a few inches shorter was blond. And the smallest one had the almond-shaped eyes of Asian ancestry. Pulling up the rear was a creamy-skinned, red-haired woman; Duchess.

Duchess' sure steps faltered when she met Beau's gaze. Beau almost allowed the woman to pretend she didn't see her. But that was ridiculous. Duchess was dating her friend, which meant that she and Beau would need to become friends as well.

Beau stood and waved to Duchess. She decided she'd imagined the grimace on the other woman's face. Duchess pulled the oldest child in. She pointed at the two younger boys. The oldest nodded and then turned his attention to his brothers. Duchess made her way to Beau and her aunt. Her smile was fragile. Her steps reluctant.

"Auntie this is the woman Darrell's dating."

"That's not what I see," said Gale squinting at the red head.

Duchess tensed.

Beau put a calming hand on Duchess' shoulder. She wanted to assure the woman that she had nothing to worry about with Darrell. Darrell was truly the perfect man. He was kind and loyal and smart. He was fabulous with kids. He had a giving soul.

Beau wanted to tell Duchess to be patient with his serious exterior, because there was a funny guy buried in there that only needed a little coaxing to come out. She wanted to tell her that under Darrell's hands she would find peace and strength. That Darrell was a true partner who would seek her opinion and help her carry out any task.

"Hello, Ms. Charmayne," Duchess said.

"Hello, my dear Ducky. It's been too long."

Beau looked between the two. "You two know each other?"

"Don't you remember, Isabeau? Her sister dated your cousin Jude when you all were younger. How is Countess?"

"She's well," said Duchess. "Thank you for asking."

Beau stared hard at Duchess, but recognition did not dawn. Her cousin Jude had dated a lot of girls in high school. He dated a lot of women now. She couldn't keep up. "I'm sorry, I don't remember you."

Duchess shrugged. "We didn't exactly run in the same circles back then."

"Well, let's change that now." Beau offered Duchess her most welcoming smile.

"You don't have to do that." Duchess shook her head. "Darrell and I are no longer together."

"What? Wait, no."

"We broke up last night."

"But I saw the two of you in my dreams. You're supposed to be together forever."

Duchess' shoulders tightened. She took a step back from Beau. She looked around as though eyeing a quick retreat.

"Remember what I told you, Isabeau," said Gale. "Dreams should never be taken literally."

Beau looked at her aunt with a question in her gray gaze. Had Gale told her that before? She would have remembered something so important. She'd leapt into Philip's arms because she'd seen him in a dream; even though it had been hazy. But she'd seen Darrell there, and Duchess, too. She'd seen so many people in her dream garden that had gotten together, and still were together to this day.

Beau turned to Duchess. "What happened?"

Duchess flinched at Beau's accusatory tone.

"I'm sorry," Beau said. "But Darrell's such a great guy. And the two of you together makes sense."

"Now, now." Gale moved past Beau to take Duchess' hand and led her to the bench. The two of them sat, leaving Beau standing, dumbfounded.

Gale wrapped an arm around Duchess' tense shoulder. And like most people did, Duchess poured her heart out to Gale.

"I have a habit of choosing men who aren't interested in me. My ex-husband..." She opened her mouth but no words escaped. Her eyes went to her children playing happily on the slide with Flora and Buck.

Duchess stared at them and the words fell out of her mouth. "He was abusive. And not just to me. It took longer than it should have, but I got me and the kids out of there. I thought I'd learned from my mistakes and that I was making better decisions. But I fell right back into my old patterns of choosing someone who didn't actually want me."

"But Darrell is interested in you," Beau insisted. "He told me so himself. And I saw you in my dreams. The people who come together in my dreams always stay together."

Duchess looked at Beau, doubt rimming her light eyes. "Darrell is more interested in you. Whenever we were together the conversation always made its way around to you."

"Really?" Beau breathed. Then she refocused on the lecture at hand. Darrell and Duchess had to get back together. She'd seen it in her dreams. If they weren't meant to be, then… She couldn't even think it.

"What my marriage taught me is that those documents don't mean anything if your heart isn't in it," Duchess said. "I gave my husband everything, more than he deserved. And I got this for my troubles."

She lifted the collar of her shirt and showed them a long and jagged scar.

"I wanted to be loved so much that I tried to fit my circular self into his square peg. When I got home from the hospital, I told myself that I wouldn't pretend anymore."

Duchess opened her arms as her youngest ran into them. He gave her a hug. Then he reached his face up for a kiss. After the peck on his mother's cheek, the child took off again.

Tears glistened in Duchess' eyes. "I know what real love looks like. I won't settle for anything less again."

She looked pointedly at Beau. "I live in reality, with my head out of the clouds and my feet on the ground. I can't afford to do anything else."

Duchess squeezed Gale's hand. Then she got up from the bench to join her patchwork family, leaving Beau staring after them. Duchess chased after the youngest, who ran through a small patch of flowers. The grin on both mother and son's face awakened an ache deep inside of Beau.

25

"Check mate. That was a pretty easy block. Are you feeling okay, Dr. Darrell?"

Darrell blinked and looked down at the chessboard. Seth had taken him out in only five moves, or maybe it was four. His mind was elsewhere. "I'm sorry, Seth. I've got a lot on my mind today."

"Women problems?"

Darrell raised his eyebrows. He opened his mouth, unsure of what was about to come out. But it didn't matter because the ten-year-old boy kept talking.

"I gave my heart to Kimmei. Did I tell you we wrote a song together? I gave her dragons, and she left me for another city."

Darrell nodded at the boy while staring down at the pawn in his hand. Duchess hadn't returned any of his phone calls. Not calls; call. He'd only made one. He didn't want to be a bother.

"Kimmei's off living her dream and I'm here playing chess."

One of the reasons Darrell hadn't made more than one

call to Duchess was because he didn't want to defend himself against her accusations about his feelings for Beau. Because if he was honest, there were some feelings there that were a bit more than friendly.

"What are we gonna do, Dr. Darrell?"

"About what?" Darrell focused again on the young boy.

"About these girls leaving us behind and breaking our hearts? Maybe we should just give up on love."

Beau's face popped into Darrell's mind's eye. In his mind, she was asleep. Her heart-shaped face was relaxed. Her lush lips slanted in a slight smile. Her long lashes kissed the tops of her cheeks. With her eyes closed, Darrell was able to look his fill. His fingertips tingled like the remnants of an electric charge. But he didn't feel the need to get closer or touch. Only look. He wanted to watch over her peace. He wanted to guard her well being.

"No," he said to Seth. "We can't give up on love."

"But doesn't it hurt? When they don't love you back?"

"Yeah, it does." Darrell felt hollowness in his chest when he thought of Beau. It was nothing like what he'd felt when he'd lost Pumpkin. It didn't compare to the loss of Duchess.

"What do we do about it?" Seth asked.

Darrell looked into the intelligent brown eyes of the young boy before him. Seth's eyes were wide and eager, waiting for instruction from his mentor. Only, Darrell had no clue what move to make.

"Well, talking to you helped me feel a little better," Seth said. "Maybe that's what we do. We talk to our friends. I'm glad you're still my friend, Dr. Darrell. Even though my mom married Manny. I'm glad Manny's my friend too. He's good to talk to."

Darrell leaned back in his chair and stared at the empty

wall across from him. Manny had been a great friend to talk to. But they hadn't spoken in a year.

"You're welcome to talk to me any time."

Darrell turned to see Manny Charmayne standing in the doorway to the game room.

"Both of you," Manny said as he eyed Darrell.

Darrell noticed that the man looked happy. It was as though Darrell could see the glow around Manny that he said he'd seen around Pumpkin. Looking into Manny's glowing face, Darrell felt the hollowness in his chest lift. He ached to tell his old friend all that had gone down in the past couple of weeks. But he didn't. He couldn't. His feelings were still hurt from the betrayal, and his pride smarted.

But why did his pride smart? He had never been in love with Pumpkin. He saw now that it never would've worked out for them. Sure, she'd met everything on his list. But just like with Duchess, there hadn't been a spark between them. They could've lived a passionless, safe life. But now that Darrell had felt the spark that they all talked about, he knew he could never play it safe again.

Manny sighed in the face of Darrell's silence. He gave a resigned nod of his head. It was unlike the man, thought Darrell. Manny was a go-getter, a charmer. Why was he giving Darrell so much space? Why wasn't he fighting to mend their friendship? Wasn't he worth it?

Suddenly, anger boiled in Darrell.

"Seth," said Darrell rising. "Why don't you go to the coat room and get your backpack. I want to have a word with your stepfather."

"Okay," Seth went out of the room without a care.

Manny's gaze went wary. "Pumpkin's busy, otherwise she would've come. I guess I should've called Gale, but I thought... maybe?"

Manny gave Darrell a sidelong glance. He narrowed his eyes, searching the other man's face. Darrell supposed he didn't find what he was looking for, because he let out a long sigh.

"I've been trying to give you your space, like everyone says I should," Manny continued. "But it's been a year. Don't you think it's time we talked?"

"You haven't come and talked to me because everyone said stay away?"

"Yeah; Pumpkin, Gale. They said you wouldn't listen until you found love yourself. And then Beau…"

Darrell tensed at the mention of her name.

"…Beau said you were dating. So I thought… maybe? Maybe it's time that I could come and talk with you. We were friends once."

"I would've never betrayed you like you did me." Apparently, some of the old hurt was still there.

"The way Pumpkin and I did things was wrong," Manny conceded. "You deserved better. When I saw her, and she had that gold around her, I just stopped thinking straight." Manny's eyes went hazy with the memory. A smile tugged at his lip.

"But you had feelings for her before that?" said Darrell.

Manny winced as he waggled his head in a nod that bounced around his shoulders. "I liked her. I liked her a lot. I was attracted to her, too. I'll admit that."

Darrell had been attracted to Beau the moment he saw her. Despite himself, he liked her. He liked her a lot. He could admit that now.

"But I kept my hands to myself once I knew you were seeing her," Manny continued. "You're an important part of my life, Darrell. But she's my world. It took me a minute, but then I saw that in the blink of an eye."

Darrell understood what he meant. When he saw the ring on Beau's finger, he'd kept his hands to himself —figuratively speaking. But then, in such a short manner of time his world had come to revolve around Beau. Beau and her health. Beau and her children. When would he see Beau next? Was Beau sleeping well?

"I see you understand that now," Manny tested out a smile towards him. "You've found the one for you."

Darrell's chin dropped to his chest. His eyes found the floor. Because he did understand. He'd found the one for him. Only she could never be his.

Manny chuckled. "It knocks you down, doesn't it? And Ducky's a red-head, full of fire, I'll bet. But that's not how I remember her from high school."

Darrell frowned, realizing Manny was talking about Duchess. "No, Duchess and I..."

"You two didn't make up last night?" Manny grimaced. "Just give it some time. It's supposed to heal all wounds."

Darrell shook his head. "No. Not this time. We're not meant to be."

Manny frowned. "But I thought Beau saw you with her in a dream?"

"Beau was wrong. There's someone else."

Manny pursed his lips and shrugged. "Gale used to tell Beau not to take her dreams so literally. Did you know that's why she married her husband? I'm not Philip's biggest fan. A mismatch if ever I saw one."

"I'm not a fan either," said Darrell. "He barely helps her. She's so tired all the time. The reason she hasn't been sleeping is because she's always so exhausted and stressed. And then the kids. Faun was emulating his father, throwing fits, expecting his mom to do everything, and being mean to his sister. All he needed, all that all of them needed, was just a little attention and care."

Darrell stopped his tirade to see that Manny was staring at him. He knew that those gray eyes saw more in his words than he'd meant to communicate.

"Oh, D," Manny sighed.

Darrell squared his shoulders, but he didn't deny it.

"If it had been six years ago, I would've pushed you into her arms," Manny said. "But today? Charmaynes don't get divorced."

"Even if it's the wrong partner?"

Manny actually tilted his head and thought about it. But he came to the same inevitable calculation and shook his head. "This is insane."

"Yes, it is. It's the definition of insanity. Doing the same thing over and over again and expecting different results. She's going to spend the rest of her life pretending she's happy because of a dream. It's crazy."

"I don't disagree with you." Manny said. "I just don't know how to make it right."

Manny reached out and rested a hand on his shoulder. The weight felt good there.

"Listen, Darrell. I know we're still on shaky ground, but if you ever want to talk..."

"Thanks... maybe... I'll call you."

Manny grinned. It was the triumphant grin of his charming, never-take-no-for-an-answer friend. He turned to go. As he went out the door, Darrell got the feeling he'd be seeing his friend again very soon. For the first time in a year, the thought brought the lightness of anticipation to his heart instead of the heavy weight of anger.

She was falling again. Falling into the dream. When her feet hit the ground she looked around, not for Philip.

For Darrell.

Beau sought out his warm strength, his gentle hand, and his calming presence. But he wasn't there. The sky was clear. The clouds were bright.

She went along the garden path. At the crest of the cliff, there stood Philip. He stood in his suit, looking out at the horizon. Beau squinted and noticed that the suit wasn't gray. It was dark blue. She wondered if it had always been dark blue and she'd just imagined it gray.

She came up to stand beside Philip. His shoulders slumped. He looked weary, like he had a lot on his mind. He was looking down at the boat.

From this vantage point, Beau saw into the boat. She saw her kids splashing in the water. She saw Gale with her skirts pulled up to her knees playing with the twins, and Seth, and a little girl with puffy hair that resembled the

Asian woman sitting next to her brother. She saw the babysitter Daeho and her blond-haired boyfriend.

There were a few of her cousins, Christian and his wife and their little girl. Chris' younger siblings, Isla and Judas, were walking alongside a lion, or was it a leopard? Aside from the visuals not making any sense, the place where her cousins were in the dream was a bit hazy.

She saw Manny and Pumpkin boarding the boat. The two were holding hands, looking as in love as ever. Manny waved to someone on the shore. It was Darrell.

Beau's heart kicked up. Her spine straightened at the sight of him. Her fingers itched to reach out to him.

But Darrell wasn't looking up at her. He was looking behind himself. At Duchess.

Standing beside her husband, Beau's shoulders slumped at the sight of Darrell smiling down at Duchess. They came closer. Darrell took Duchess' hand as she approached the boat. He said something to her and she laughed.

So much for their break up. They looked happy. They looked good together. They looked right. Whatever they were going through now was just a rough patch. Everyone Beau dreamed about stayed together.

She looked beside her at Philip. When he looked down at her, he didn't smile. He studied her face; not like a stranger would. He studied her as though he was trying to figure out if she had a new hairstyle or a new outfit.

Beau turned back to the water. The two of them should be heading down there soon. But Philip didn't look as though he was headed in that direction. His gaze was trained off into the distance.

Back down at the water's edge where her family gathered, Beau watched as Darrell let Duchess' hand go once they hit the water's edge. Her cousin, Jude, came out into the water and held out his hand to Duchess. She took it hesitantly and he helped her into the boat. The way Duchess had looked at Darrell didn't hold a candle to the way she looked at Jude. Jude's eyes held the same torch for Duchess.

Then everyone down below looked up to the cliff at her. They all waved her towards them. Darrell's smile was the hugest as he looked up at her. It drew her near. But she hesitated. She turned to look at Philip.

Philip regarded the boat with the same wariness on his face and slump in his shoulders. She reached for his hand, but felt the two of them being pulled in different directions.

Beau did not want to go the direction that Philip wanted to take her. Philip was unyielding in where he wanted to go.

Finally, Beau let go of his hand.

Philip gave her a small smile and a wave. And then he was gone.

At first, Beau panicked. She wrung her empty hands and stared at the space where he just was, where he'd always been. Slowly, the panic receded, and lightness settled over her.

A sound called her attention down below. The boat's anchor was rising. She wasn't going to make it in time. She rushed down the cliff. Darrell hopped out of the boat and ran to her. He caught her in his arms and she fell into his strength.

The sun broke through the clouds. The rays backlit Darrell, making him shine like a brown god. His eyes dipped to her lips. Beau's lips parted in response. Where she had been light a moment ago, she felt a heavy need weigh her down.

She looked into his hazel eyes and somehow knew he felt the same. But still, they both hesitated. Even in the dream they knew they were not free to do what they both desired. What they both felt they needed. What they wished was their right. And so they held on to each other, neither letting go as the boat rocked away from them.

The waters became choppy and rough. Beau tightened her grip around Darrell's neck. Something was rocking her entire body, pulling her away from him and out of the dream.

She struggled to hold on to Darrell. To hold on to this perfect peace. But the grogginess pulled at her clarity and her eyes opened.

"Beau!"

Beau looked into the face of the man she'd dreamed about, the man she'd married and spent the last six years of her life trying to please and placate. His features looked dark and stormy. There was tension in his shoulders just like in the dream. The same wariness on his face.

He wasn't calling her name like a hero searching for her on a Moorish peak. No, Philip was irritated and annoyed.

"Look, I'm glad that you've kicked the insomnia. Believe me, I'm glad that I don't have to be awakened in the night anymore by your nightmares or your kicking. But you can't sleep the day away. You've gotta take the kids to school. And then you still haven't found that video for me."

Beau sat up, staring at him. He stood there in his dark blue suit; completely dressed and put together. She heard the kids running around outside the door. They likely hadn't been given breakfast. He probably hadn't even said good morning to them. Beau suddenly felt weary. She collapsed back onto the mattress, staring at the ceiling.

How did she get here?

"Beau, get up. We can't afford for you to be lazy. We have a business to run."

Beau chuckled still staring at the ceiling. "You do understand that the word we has two letters. W and E. Exactly which one are you?"

"You're not making any sense, and I don't have time for it this morning."

"Whenever you say *we what you actually mean is *me. *I have to do this. *I have to do that. *I do everything."

"That's bullshit—"

"Which would be okay, if you actually meant we sometimes. If you actually did any of the things you told me to do."

"That I 'tell you to do'?"

He was getting riled up, but she didn't care.

"But you don't," she said. "You don't ever do anything. You go out and you play around. You make more work for me. You make decisions without me that will increase my workload when I'm already overloaded. I never get a break. Since the day I met you I haven't gotten a break."

"If you don't want to be here, then don't."

Beau stared at him again. His cheeks were puffed out like their son's when he was in the middle of a tantrum. His arms were crossed at his chest. His lips were pursed as though he smelled something fowl. He looked nothing like he did in her dreams.

"Do you?" she asked. "Do you want to be here? With me? With the kids."

His face looked incredulous. His mouth opened as though he were going to affirm such a ludicrous question. Then his jaw tensed.

"Are you happy, Philip?"

Again no answer, only more tensing. This time in the shoulders.

"Did you actually want any of this?" she asked.

"I did the right thing," he said tensely. "I married you when you found out you were pregnant. I went into this business and tried to make the best out of it. I've been loyal to this marriage."

Beau sat up. Her spine immediately protested the decision, but she did it anyway. "I think we're cheating on each other."

He stared at her, betrayal written on his handsome features.

"I think we both betrayed who we really are," she continued. "What our dreams were. I think we threw those aside to do what's right, and neither of us feels right."

Philip's facial features rearranged themselves into something Beau hadn't seen before; consideration. He uncrossed his arms from his chest and planted his fists on his hips. He tugged his lower lip into his mouth as he contemplated her words.

"Are you happy, Philip?" she asked again. "Because I'm not. I haven't been happy in a long time. I think we make each other unhappy. I think we punish each other because of it. And I think we do it because we blame each other. We need to stop blaming each other for not reaching our dreams."

"What do you want to do?" he said. "Go to counseling or something?" He sighed, more tension in his shoulders at yet another potential burden.

Beau reached out for his hand. He took a tentative step towards her and then gave her his hand. She rubbed at the gold band on his finger.

"I think we should change course." Beau released his hand. "I think we should let each other go."

He took his hand back and blinked at her. His eyes scrunched in confusion.

"I think we should separate, and figure out what we truly want and then go after it."

"What exactly are you saying, Isabeau?"

"I want a divorce."

27

"You just have one more patient for the day, Dr. Walker. A walk-in. Here's the chart."

Darrell looked down at the clipboard. He took a deep inhalation as he read the name on the file. His fingers tingled as they held the sheets of paperwork in his hands. "Thanks, Michelle. Why don't you take off. I can close up after this."

"You sure?" she asked, but she already had her back to him, packing her bag.

"Of course," Darrell grinned. "Go home to your family."

"Thanks, Doctor D."

Darrell waited for her to grab her coat and exit before he walked over to the door to the exam room.

"Hi." Beau stood on the other side of the door.

"What are you doing here?" he asked as he closed the door behind him.

He took her in. She wore a flower-printed sundress and flats. Her dark hair was loose around her shoulders. Her form took his breath, but her face confused him.

Her eyes were wide, as though she'd been startled. Her

lips were full and pouty. Her hands were at her heart, and she wrung them as though she were nervous.

"Are you hurt?" he asked. He was on her before she could answer. His eyes doing a visual assessment of the symmetry of her shoulder blades. He needed to get his hands on her spine to ensure its alignment.

"I'm fine," she said.

Her head was tilted back as she looked up at him. Darrell smelled something sweet on her breath. He saw the creases in her lips where her lip-gloss missed a crack. He saw a dollop of eyeliner where her lashes were clumped together. Even with her imperfections she was still perfect. Then he realized the reason he could see these things was because he was standing so close to her.

"I was hoping I could catch you before you left the office," she said, not backing out of their close proximity. Her eyes were fastened to his chest as though it were her favorite pillow. "Can we talk?"

"Are you sure you're feeling okay?" Darrell itched to get his hands on her, and an adjustment was the only way he knew to do it.

"I'm fine," she insisted. "I'm a healed woman thanks to you."

"So, you're not here for an adjustment?" he said. "You're here as a friend?"

"I..." she began, then stopped. "I had another dream."

Darrell wasn't sure if he could handle a friendly chat with Beau about her dream man and her dream life. He felt a twinge in his low back at the prospect.

"You were there," she said. "Everyone was there. My entire family, the kids, even some people I didn't know, but I guess I'll meet soon."

She smiled with a far off look. Darrell took a step closer

to her. There were no bags under her eyes. She was standing straight, her shoulders were level. She was doing well. She looked happy, truly happy, and he couldn't be upset about it. He wanted to taste that smile on her lips.

"But you…" Beau took a step closer to him.

"I…" Darrell took another step.

"We…" Beau met him toe to toe.

"You and I?" He was embarrassed at the hope in his voice. His friend was coming to him for help, and he was hoping for more than she could ever give to him. He stared down at the ring on her finger.

Wait? Where was her ring?

"You were going to kiss me," she said.

He jerked back, putting distance between the two of them. He shook his head in denial. At least he thought he shook his head. It felt like his entire body was shaking with want.

"In the dream," she clarified. "You were about to kiss me in the dream. We were about to kiss each other. God, it was so real. I felt your arms around me and I felt so safe. You made me feel strong and protected at the same time."

They were treading dangerous ground and Darrell knew it. When her hand landed on his chest he knew he wouldn't remove it. "Beau…"

"I felt the softness of your lips. I smelled your breath." Her hands moved across his heart.

Darrell reached for the only thing that made sense. Facts. "Dreams are a series of thoughts, images, and sensations that—"

"I'm getting a divorce."

He was hallucinating now.

"I asked my husband for a divorce."

He ran the words over and over in his head.

"I realized that he may have been in my dream," she continued. "But he's not the one I want. I never felt like this in my dreams. Not like how I feel with you. God, you don't even know that I have feelings for you. Do you? *Hey, Darrell, it turns out I have feelings for you.*"

She said it without much care. She was the type of woman who wasn't afraid of her feelings. Because she was the type of woman who had never been rejected.

"I'm sorry. I'm just now realizing this might come as a shock to you." She stepped away from him, her head low, her gaze averted. "God, what was I thinking? It never even occurred to me that you might not feel the same way. I am an idiot."

No, he realized. Isabeau Rumpel Rosen had never met with rejection in her life and she wouldn't meet with it now.

"Beau, no." He paused, thinking of something else to say. "No," was all he could come up with.

"I just saw us together in a dream and I thought..." she huffed. "I didn't think. I just acted. I haven't learned my lesson. Dreams aren't always what they seem. You've probably never even thought of me like that."

Darrell had never been one for words, but he knew a great deal of them. He was never at a loss for them. Usually the right ones never came out at the right time. Now none would come out at all.

"I've just jeopardized our friendship, haven't I? That's the last thing I wanted to do." She scrubbed her hands over her face. The edge of her palms came away with black smudges, and still she was beautiful. "Just forget I said anything."

She stepped around him and headed for the door. Now, not only was his tongue tied, Darrell's feet were immovable.

He opened his mouth wide, but sound eluded him. He reached for her, but she was beyond his grasp.

She turned. "I just need you to know that I didn't come to this decision out of the blue. It was sudden —yes— but I'm sure. I never felt like this in reality with Philip; how I feel with you. You make me feel like I can do anything. And then when I'm uncertain, you raise me up. That's how I want my life to be, Darrell. I want to be a we, and not an I."

"Beau..." But his voice croaked out barely above a whisper. Even if she heard him, she didn't stop. She was on a roll.

"I want you to know that I think the world of you. That I see you are the most decent, thoughtful, kind, compassionate, and amazing man I've ever met; I want to be something more to you. But I know I'm not entitled to it. My dreams aren't what they seem. I saw Duchess with you and then with my cousin Jude. I saw my cousin Isla with a lion, for god's sake"

"Beau."

The sound of his voice broke through her monologue. She stopped talking and faced him. There was uncertainty and vulnerability written all over her face.

"I have feelings for you, too," he admitted.

"You do?"

All logic went out the window. Now that he was hearing the words, he could finally admit to himself that this was all that mattered; being someone's number one. She was choosing him. Finally, the woman he wanted was choosing him.

"I do," he confirmed. With his voice freed, one of his feet unrooted and he took a step towards her.

"It's over between Philip and me." She took a step toward him.

"Duchess broke up with me." His other foot unrooted and drew him closer to her.

"Philip moved out last night. It was a dream with him." She closed the remaining distance between them. "I want the reality I have with you. But I'm happy to start with dinner."

Darrell looked into those light gray eyes and saw forever. For the first time in his life, he wanted to throw all caution to the wind. He didn't know who moved first, but their lips came together.

She tasted like his every wet dream. Her soft lips put to shame every pinup girl fantasy. Her soft sighs put to shame every love song ever written.

"It's just like in my dream," Beau breathed when they came up for air.

"Mine, too."

He captured her lips again. His tongue traced the seams of her mouth. He didn't expect her to open for him, knew she probably shouldn't. She'd only spoken of divorce. The bond between her and her husband was still there legally, if not spiritually. If not in her heart. If not in her mind. If not in her soul.

Beau opened for him. When her tongue tasted the underside of his top lip, it captured his spirit. When her teeth nipped at his bottom lip, she stole his heart and mind. The breath she exchanged with him told him he had her soul.

They stumbled farther into the room, until the back of his legs met with the exam table. It was sturdy enough for what he wanted to do to her. All he had to do was sit back and pull her thighs over him.

He felt Beau's leg riding up his. Darrell broke the kiss

and turned his head to catch a clean breath of air, not tainted with the sweet, intoxicating essence of her.

"We can't," he said.

"No, we can't," she agreed. "Not yet." She rested her head on his chest. She tilted her head up and into the crook of his neck and she inhaled. Then she let out a contented sigh.

Darrell sat down on the exam table. He had to. The weight of her serenity overwhelmed him. He vowed he would do any and everything to keep that feeling cloaked around her.

Darrell wrapped Beau in his arms and pulled her into him. She stood between his thighs and gave him the rest of her weight.

"This is enough for me," he said. "You're everything I ever wanted."

"I made your list?"

"You *are* my list."

She giggled, curling her hand into his chest. "I want to do this right. I don't want any strings attached to me when I throw myself at you. You should know, on our first date, you're gonna get lucky."

He laughed and pulled her in closer. "I *am* lucky.

He'd wrap himself around her if he could. And soon, he would be able to.

28

On the drive home, Beau felt the trill of the engine in her core as she moved along the street. Inside her chest and all down her spine, she felt the hum of Darrell's love as its after-effects continued to spread through her body. Who knew a couple, okay more than a couple, of kisses could ignite such a huge flame and keep it burning for so long after.

A horn honked. Beau jerked her attention back to the streets. The guy in front of her leaned on his horn as she swerved back into her lane. The truck driver glared at her as he zoomed past her car.

Beau squinted at the truck. It had a huge spinning wheel and sheep on its side. She blinked as she turned her head forward and tried to catch another glimpse in the rearview mirror. Was that the same truck that had hit her before?

Did the truck have a vendetta out for her, or something? But that was silly. She was having silly thoughts after such amazing attention.

She'd known Darrell was a magician with his hands

when he'd only been interested in her spine. Now that he had full access to her body he'd proven he was masterful. They'd kept everything above the waist, for now. But soon, the good doctor would have a free pass. Just as soon as she and Philip made their separation official.

Philip. She didn't want to think about him right now. Technically she was still married, even though they'd agreed to get the divorce. Philip had had her loyalty for years but he hadn't had her heart in a long time.

Truly, he'd never had it. She'd thrown herself at him based on a dream. She wasn't doing that now with Darrell. Whether she dreamed about Darrell again or not, she knew that she wanted the reality she had with him.

She pulled up to her house and didn't see DaeHo's car, or rather DaeHo's boyfriend's car. Tyler had dropped DaeHo off when she'd come over to sit the kids for Beau while she raced off to see Darrell. When the two teens came inside, Tyler had made no move to leave. Beau hadn't minded. Young love was precious.

In the place of Tyler's car, she saw Philip's car. She wasn't expecting him home. She had to replace that word in her mind. This was no longer his home. They'd agreed she would keep the house and the kids. She didn't think for a second there would be a fight over either. They would leave the rest to lawyers. He could have whatever he wanted.

Beau found her soon-to-be-ex sitting in the living room. He was looking straight ahead at the dark television screen. His skin looked pale in the dim light. His chiseled cheeks looked as though they'd sunk into his jowls.

"Philip? Is everything okay? I thought you were gone for the weekend."

His eyes were as wide as an owl's when he turned to her.

"Something came up. I let the sitter go home early. We need to talk."

"Mommy," Flora ran into the room. "Ms. Dae read us the story of *Little Red Riding Hood*."

"And Mr. Ty did the wolf sounds," said Buck with a huge grin on his face. "I can do them, too. You wanna hear?"

"Not now." Philip's voice was sharp.

Buck's smile fell and his eyes slapped down to the ground, like blinds being shuttered. Beau shot Philip daggers. She got down on her children's level.

"Guys, I'll come to your room and we'll read the story again. You can be the wolf through the whole story, Buck. But first I'm going to have a chat with daddy, okay?"

Flora nodded. Buck didn't answer. The little boy turned and sulked down the hall.

"Everything's going to be okay, daddy." Flora approached her father but didn't hug him. Instead, she rubbed him on the kneecap.

Beau saw so much of herself in the little girl. She'd spent so many years trying to calm Philip down and salve his upsets. She hated that her daughter inherited that. But she would no longer be modeling that behavior. Both Flora and Buck would get to see what a true partnership looked like when they saw her and Darrell together.

She wondered when it would be appropriate to let the children know that she was now seeing Darrell. Hell, she and Philip hadn't even told them that they were getting a divorce. They'd have to talk about when and how to sit the kids down and do that.

The thought was daunting, and she didn't have anyone she could turn to for advice. There'd never been a divorce in the Charmayne family. She'd be the first. But she would not allow that fact to deter her from her happiness. She and

Philip were not meant to continue this particular journey together. They'd always be co-parents. They just would no longer be co-partners. They'd never truly been partners.

Once the kids went down the hall, Beau followed Philip into the home office. "What the hell is wrong with you?"

"Where have you been?" In the bright office light, he didn't look well. There was sweat on his brow, a manic look in his eyes. His shirt was disheveled.

"I was out with a friend."

She held her breath waiting for him to ask her to clarify, wondering if she was about to tell Philip a lie. She wasn't ready to tell him that she was already seeing someone else. But she decided she wouldn't lie. She wasn't ashamed of her relationship with Darrell. It was the best thing in her life next to the kids. Philip would find out soon enough that she'd moved on.

"I've been calling your phone and you haven't answered."

Beau felt in her pockets. No phone. She looked down in her purse and it wasn't in its compartment. She must've left it in the car or at Darrell's. Instead of being worried, she was excited that she had an excuse to go and see him again sooner than they'd planned.

"We have a problem," Philip said.

Beau's hackles went up at that one word. She ignored the other three. Outside of the children there was no more "we" between her and Philip. Whatever problem he had was his alone.

"We're being investigated," he said.

"You keep saying we," Beau said. "There is no we any longer, Philip."

"There's a reporter who's been calling me. They're investigating Yohance Stanley. There have been a lot of complaints lately. The items he's sent to the needy are faulty and cheap."

"He's raised hundreds of thousands for us in a matter of weeks," Beau said. "Why would he send cheap items?"

"I don't know?" Philip shrugged. "To save money? It seemed smart at the time. But now, there are reports that his callers are preying on the elderly and mentally ill. One report said that callers targeted a woman with dementia, and had her put donations on her credit card totaling $10,000."

Beau turned green. She collapsed onto one of the office chairs. Hadn't Manny warned her of this? "Philip, what have you done?"

"This isn't my fault." He rounded on her, lips pursed like a petulant child. He slumped down in the chair across from her. "I kept telling you to look into Stanley. You never did. You would've seen something like this."

Beau looked over at Philip. She looked at him with clear eyes. She looked at Philip now and remembered all the times that, instead of leaving him to solve the problem, she'd taken it out of his hands. She thought of all the times she'd shushed his tantrums, just like she did with their son. He was right. She would have seen something like this. Because deep down, she would never have trusted him with this much responsibility.

If she'd been well, she would've investigated Yohance Stanley and learned all of these atrocities before they could hurt her business. If she hadn't been hit by a truck, she would've seen this problem coming her way and saved her husband and her family from this disaster.

She knew what the old Beau would do. That woman would tell her husband that everything would be okay. That she would take on the weight of this task and handle the matter.

But she wasn't that woman any longer. She wasn't going to do that now. It had been a mistake to do it in the past. It was a mistake to do it with Buck now. Darrell had shown her that. Buck needed to learn to solve his own problems. He needed positive reinforcement and support along the way. And that's exactly what his father needed, too.

"Philip, everything will be okay."

She closed her eyes when she realized she sounded just like Flora trying to soothe a situation with a sunny attitude, kind words, and a pat on the knee. Beau had made so many mistakes, not only with her husband, but with her children. No more. Things were changing from this moment on.

"I'll be here to support you through this," she said. "But you made this decision. You're going to have to figure it out for yourself."

Philip grimaced. He jerked his knee away from her.

Beau continued with the tough love. "You're going to have to face the consequences, if there are any. I'll be here to stand by you and support you."

"What do you mean *I* will face the consequences? You're my wife. You're my partner. You're going to help me fix this."

Beau leaned back in her chair. The warm glow that had spread throughout her body only an hour before, in Darrell's arms, turned cold. She would give anything to still be there in his office, held securely in his embrace, while his hands roamed her back.

"*We're* going to fix this," he said.

"There is no more *we*, Philip."

He shook his head. "If *I* go down, we go down. And if *we* go down, then those reporters, and maybe the authorities, will look into your family. There might be implications for Charmayne Charities and the mayor's office."

Beau felt the darkness closing in on her as she stared into his crystal blue eyes.

"We have to present a united front. Otherwise they'll know something's wrong," Philip said. "The divorce is off."

29

The sun looked brighter. The sky was a cloudless blue. Darrell swore he saw stars twinkle at him from the bright sky, as the sun went down. Birds chirped overhead. He felt like he was walking in a fairytale. Like he was a character in a Disney Technicolor spectacular. All he needed was for a horse to gallop into the frame.

The sound of a loud muffler had Darrell turning to look over his shoulder. A white Mustang pulled up to the curb. The silver horse on the front end gleamed like a grin under the streetlights. Manny hopped out and joined Darrell at the entrance to the bar.

Darrell had agreed to meet Manny for drinks, but that was before he'd spent the prior evening making out with his married cousin in an exam room. Just thinking back to it made Darrell's steps slow and a grin spread across his face.

Having Beau in his arms had been like a homecoming. His body had been alive with each touch, each kiss. He may not have seen gold, but he finally understood what everyone meant when they said they fell in love. It had been a wonderful, painless fall that Darrell would be happy to take a running leap and do over and over again.

He was in love. It was undeniable. He looked at Manny as he sat beside him on a barstool. If this was how he felt the first time he'd kissed Pumpkin, Darrell could never be mad at the man... ever again.

"There's going to be a new marriage in the Rumpel clan."

Darrell blinked. Had Beau already told her cousin about their relationship? Had she leaped over dating and straight to marriage? After all the dates Darrell had been on over the past year, he should be breaking out in hives. But he wasn't. A sense of joy spread through his chest at the thought of Isabeau Walker.

"I can't believe Guy is finally getting hitched!"

"Who?" Darrell frowned.

"Beau's brother," explained Manny. "You met him before. In fact, it was the same day you met me. Remember?"

Darrell did not remember.

"It was at my cousin, Jude's, beach party."

Darrell did remember Judas Charmayne. The two men had been in school together. Judas had the family charm, but the two hadn't connected like he and Manny had. The last Darrell had heard of Judas was that he had a successful plastic surgery practice in New Orleans.

"Anyway," Manny continued at Darrell's lapse of memory, "I was beginning to think that Guy would never find the One. I think he thought it, too. But just when you've given up, that's when love hits you."

Darrell swished his drink around in his glass. He'd been looking for love. He'd been looking for it actively, calculatingly, scientifically. It had crept up on him in a way that he couldn't quantify or make logical sense of. He knew it was real. He knew it was true.

"I hope that smile's for the red-head," said Manny.

Darrell hadn't realized he was grinning. Now that he was paying attention, he felt the tug at each of the corners of his mouth. He felt the tug of his bottom lip in his teeth. He felt the lashes touch the tops of his cheeks as his eyes briefly closed to reveal a vision of Beau. Her eyes closed, her lips swollen from their shared kisses, her head tilted back, asking for more.

"Darrell?"

Darrell opened his eyes slowly. He didn't meet Manny's questioning gaze. The long sigh told Darrell that Manny saw the truth. And he should see the truth. Everyone would see the truth before long.

He and Beau weren't hiding anything. Of course, they'd take their time before they began shouting their feelings from the rooftop. He knew that divorces were a lengthy, messy, emotional process. But this thing was happening.

"I'm with Beau." Darrell held up his hand before Manny could state the obvious. "She won't be married for long. She's getting a divorce. She's unhappy. I know you can see that."

Manny didn't say anything. He chewed at his lower lip and glared at Darrell. They hadn't spoken in nearly a year. In the years that they had known each other it was usually Darrell counseling Manny on his oft-questionable decisions with women.

"I make her happy," Darrell insisted. "I made her dream again. She saw me in a dream."

It was the best proof he could come up with. Darrell knew he sounded crazy. Only, Manny wasn't looking at him like he was crazy. He was looking at him with empathy.

"I love her," Darrell continued. "We didn't plan this. I tried to ignore it, but it knocked me off my feet. I'm going to take care of her and put a smile on her face for the rest of my life. She's everything I ever imagined. Everything I didn't dare to hope for."

And she seemed to be everywhere, not just in his thoughts. She was on the television screen above the bar. She stood by a man who looked very much like her husband, though Darrell had only seen the man once.

Darrell squinted at the television screen. It was unmistakably Beau. But this could've been old newsreel footage. They were Saint Anne's royalty after all. Then he saw that the coverage said "live."

The headline read: Rosens Stand Firm as Charity Comes Under Fire.

"Is that Beau?" Manny peered around Darrell.

"Turn that up," Darrell shouted to the bartender.

The volume rose louder over the hum of the bar. Darrell hopped off his bar stool and moved closer.

"My wife and I will defeat these charges," said Philip Rosen. "We have done nothing wrong. Our business, like our marriage, is strong. Our foundation was created out of the love we have for each other. The love we vowed to share with our community. There is nothing corrupt in our business. Like our love, we'll see this through and come out the other side stronger."

Philip Rosen looked over at Beau. Her eyes were glued straight ahead to the camera. Darrell felt as though she were looking right at him. She wasn't smiling, not really. It was the fake smile, the professional smile. The same smile he'd seen the first day he met her; the smile that begged for help.

Darrell took another step, preparing to leave, to find her

and take her away from that man. But then Beau blinked. She looked away from the camera, and into the eyes of her husband. She opened her mouth. Was that his imagination or did her lips quiver.

"My husband and I are prepared to fight these allegations," she said. "We have nothing to hide."

Darrell felt everything around him go black. He heard someone calling his name. It sounded so far away. He felt a hand on his back. It felt light years away.

Darrell watched Beau walk off the screen with her arm in her husband's. She did not break free of it and run. Darrell felt as though everything fell away from him.

Beau wrenched herself awake and out from the dark tendrils of sleep. Her eyes slammed open to the glaring twilight. Her arms flew out to ward off the cloying shadows. Her chest heaved in shallow pants and her fingers curled around the empty air. Her eyes took long to adjust to the darkness that shone bright in the room.

There was bile on her tongue, mixed with the metallic tint of iron. She reached her cold, shaking fingers to her lip. They came away wet. Her eyes saw the contrast of the dark blood on her pale fingertips. She glanced up at her surroundings.

Nothing looked familiar.

Where was she?

She took a deep breath, but her tight chest protested, only allowing one tiny puff of air at a time through its constricted channels. It left her dizzy, as the four walls continued to crush in on her with the ever-growing darkness.

This was wrong, her mind whispered. Her restless legs tingled; eager to get up and run. Her churning stomach insisted she wasn't supposed to be here in this place; this cold dark place...

Her eyes slammed open. She checked the clock. It was midnight. She'd crawled into bed after the interview. Her whole body had been weary, as though she'd run back-to-back marathons.

She felt as though she'd been hit by a truck. Her shoulders were tense. She felt pressure in her head, and felt a weight on her neck. It was as though her body went through the crash again, but this time she'd never been to Darrell and felt the healing power of his hands.

Beau rolled over in the bed. Philip hadn't dared to enter their bedroom. He understood that their relationship was only for the cameras. He'd moved into the spare bedroom and had fallen soundly asleep after the interview. She knew, because she'd heard him snoring softly after she'd checked in on the kids.

Philip could sleep soundly because he no longer had a care in the world. Beau had begun looking into the dealings of Yohance Stanley. What she found turned her stomach. The man's shade went beyond the immoral methods his callers used to extract money from seniors and those with mental health disorders. He'd been under investigation for taking multiple salaries. There were a host of family members on the firm's payroll, and more luxurious company cars than she could count. She didn't know how she was going to get them out of this mess, but she would. She had no choice.

Beau sat up in her bed. Her neck protested the movement. She swung her legs out of the bed. A dull ache settled in her low spine. She needed relief and she knew the only place she could get it. She dressed and headed out the front door.

As she drove across town, she called Darrell again for the twentieth time. She'd found her phone on the floor of her car. Unfortunately, Darrell wasn't picking up. She knew he must have seen the press conference. He would've seen her standing beside Philip. She had to tell him that it was all for show, just until she could figure out this mess and disentangle the foundation from the grime of Yohance Stanley.

Before she'd left his office the other day, she and Darrell had planned their first date. It was to be at his home. He was going to make her dinner. Philip had never cooked a day in his life. She'd been so excited about the prospect of a man cooking for her.

She pulled up at Darrell's town house and saw Manny's car in the driveway. She took a deep breath before she got out of the car. When she knocked on Darrell's door, Manny answered. Her cousin grimaced when he opened the door and saw her.

"Looks like you two made up," she said.

"Yeah." Manny pulled the door closed behind him, shutting her out.

Light gray eyes slammed into Beau, hard as steel. Manny was the cousin she was closest to in the Charmayne brood; closer even than Isla, who was her nearest female cousin in age. Manny's eyes spoke volumes at her.

"Can I talk to him?" Beau said.

"I don't think that's a good idea, Beau Beau. For so many reasons. The first being that you're still wearing your wedding ring."

Beau looked down at the offending band. She put her hand behind her back. "It's not real, Manny. None of it's real."

"Darrell thought it was."

"He and I —we— are. Philip and I, none of that was

real. I was living in a dream world. I'm going to get out. I just can't yet. This scandal could hurt us all, the Charmayne Foundation included. I just need to get us out of it."

"Beau, it's not your responsibility. If Philip made this mistake then he needs to clean it up himself. You've been cleaning up after his mistakes and making excuses for him your entire relationship. That's not a marriage, it's bad parenting."

Beau was about to respond, to tell Manny that she understood that now, that she wasn't going to clean up Philip's mess. She was just trying to protect everyone else in her family. But then she saw Darrell come up behind Manny.

He looked weary. Beau had never seen him looking down. She wanted to reach out to him and crush him to her. She wanted to smooth the deep furrows in his brow and tell him that it was all going to be okay, that she would take care of everything.

"It's okay, Manny," Darrell said.

Manny looked between the two, then he threw up his hands. "I'm gonna head home," Manny said. "Let me know if you need anything? Either of you."

Manny headed to his car. Both she and Darrell watched as he turned the ignition and roared down the street.

Beau stood on the stoop and faced Darrell. "Can I come in?"

Darrell hesitated, but then he stepped back and let her pass. Before he'd closed the door she was in his arms. Every ache and pain that had assaulted her earlier melted away.

"I'm so sorry," she said. "I tried to call you, to warn you. But it all just happened so fast."

Darrell was tense inside of her embrace. But she wouldn't let go. She held on to him and kept talking.

"The last thing in the world I would ever do is hurt you," she said. "And I know that seeing that interview must've hurt you."

"It did." His voice was barely above a whisper. "I'd let myself believe..."

She pulled away so she could see his face, but didn't let him go. She knew that if she let him go, she would never get back in his arms again. So, she held on for dear life.

"It's real, Darrell. What's between us is real. All of it."

He stared at her, weighing her words.

"I don't love, Philip. I'm not sure if I ever did. I know that I wanted to, I wanted the fairytale. I talked myself into a life with him. I pretended everything was fine with him. I've never done that with you, not once. Everything between us has always been real. I didn't make it up in my head."

Darrell's face was a mask of conflict. "It didn't look real. On the television, your smile wasn't real."

Beau shook her head. "No, it wasn't. Mainly because I was thinking about you and what you would see, what you would feel; seeing Philip and me together like that, hearing what was being said."

"It felt like my heart was being ripped out."

Beau put her hand on his chest, as though she could push the organ back into place. "I'm sorry. It felt like I was ripping out my own heart; standing there in compliance."

"Why did you?"

"Philip's made some critical mistakes and we're under investigation with the charity. It could extend to the Charmayne Foundation and the community center. We just need to keep up appearances until the investigation is over."

"Appearances?"

"If I leave him, it looks like guilt."

"Are you guilty?"

"I didn't get us into this, but because I am —was— his partner, I'm guilty by association. But it's not real, Darrell. We're just pretending, just until the company is out of investigation."

She placed a hand on his cheek, the other on his back. She so much wanted to be the one to give him support during this time of strife, just as he had done with her when she was injured. She wrapped her arms around his neck and put her lips to his ear.

"I love you," she whispered.

She felt his body jerk, but she continued.

"I came to that conclusion when I was awake, so I know it's real. I know it's true. I love you, and I want to be with you."

31

*D*arrell heard the words. He watched her perfect lips form and shape each syllable. The vowels sailed to him on sighs of air. The few consonants, like the V in love, sent a shock wave straight to his heart.

She loved him. She wanted to be with him. She chose him.

She was in his arms. Her head was tilted back looking up at him. Her lips drew nearer and nearer to him.

Darrell hesitated. There was a reason he should stop her lips from getting too close to his. But for the life of him he couldn't puzzle out why. Beau's lips touched his and the pieces of the puzzle splattered.

An hour ago, Darrell hadn't believed he'd ever hold her again in his arms. He inhaled when she kissed him; soaking in her very essence. He let the taste, touch, and feel of her invade his soul. She moaned and he added sound to his collection.

One of her hands grasped the shirt fabric that covered his heart. The organ thumped hard against its cage to get to its mistress. The fingers of her other hand dug into his scalp as she pressed his head into her hungry lips. Every coherent thought bent to her will.

She loved him. She wanted to be with him. She chose him.

Finally, he was The One.

Beau was everything he'd imagined, everything he ever could've hoped for. And she stood here before him. She hadn't abandoned him. She hadn't turned her back on him. She was clinging to him, afraid to let go, as though he might run off. Didn't she know that he was wrapped around her finger?

He wrapped his hand around the fingers that had his heart. And that's when he felt it. The band was cold and the diamond sharp.

His head dipped. His shoulders caved. He shut his eyes to hold onto the dream of her. The dream of them together; the dream where he was her One and Only True Love. He let her hand go, but she wouldn't let him. She grabbed his hand back and entwined her fingers with his own. The cold of the band burned his knuckles.

"Darrell?"

He shook his head. He had to find his voice. If he didn't speak the truth, she might repeat those three little words again. *I* choose you. And then he'd be lost.

"This isn't real." Darrell opened his eyes. His heel rose to take a step back. Soft gray eyes arrested his movements. His heartbeat slowed. The air became thin. His vision fogged.

"Darrell." The consonants of his name rolled off her lips; a pillow-soft plea to stay in the dream just a little while longer.

Darrell placed his hand at the small of Beau's back. His fingers rolled and kneaded at the tension he found there.

His other hand stroked through the dark locks atop her head. Beau closed her eyes and sighed.

"I thought you were through pretending," he said.

"I am." She rested her cheek in his hand. Both of her palms rested on his heart.

"You're still pretending with him."

Her eyes opened. "I'm trying to protect everyone from him and his mistakes."

Darrell palpated her spine. He felt where she was out of alignment. He ached to lay her down on his bed and put her back together again. He stepped away from her, out of her embrace, and put his hands behind his back.

"I can't help you," he said.

Beau blinked at him. Her eyes were wide. Her mouth parted in a silent O. She looked lost, alone. She reminded him of little Flora in need of a hug or just a kind word.

"That's not true," he amended. "I could help you. I could stand by your side. I could soothe every ache that pain-in-the-ass causes you."

"Please," she said.

He shut his eyes. "This is not your fault, Beau."

"I know that." She closed the distance between them.

Darrell stepped around her. His resolve was strong, but his flesh was weak. "You need to let him clean up his own mess."

She rocked back on her heels. Her hands rose, as though to ward off an oncoming storm. "He could make an even bigger mess unless I step in. He could hurt others."

"People get hurt sometimes. Wounds heal if you let them breathe. They'll fester if you keep smothering them with good intentions."

Her hands balled and settled on her hips. She reminded him of Super Girl looking down over the helpless mortals of her city. He didn't know whether to tie a cape around her shoulders and watch her fly, or whip out some kryptonite to make her see her limitations. In the end, he did the only thing he could. He brought her back into his arms.

"I can't save you," he said into her hair. "Trust me, I would if I could. I'd jump on a horse and slay that damned dragon you call your husband. But Beau, you're gonna have to save yourself from him."

"That's what I'm trying to do."

Her lips brushed against the underside of his chin as she said the words. He nearly caved. He could have her right now. He didn't have to wait. He could sweep her off her feet and carry her into his bedroom. He could strip her down and sink into what he knew was his.

Darrell unwound Beau's fingers from his shirt. He stepped back and held her at arm's length. "When you try to do everything yourself, you wind up getting hurt. I'm not going to participate in that pattern."

She opened her mouth to protest, but he halted her with a shake of his head.

"If this is what you think you need to do, you do it," he said. "I am so far in love with you that I would stand in the shadows and wait for you to glance my way."

"I *do* love you." She stole back inside his embrace and he let her.

"I don't doubt it." His arms instinctively went to her low back. Her hands came back to rest at his heart. It seemed to be their normal way of being. "I can't remember how to not feel this way."

"Neither can I," she said. "It's like we're two puzzle pieces and we fit right together. I heard us click into place."

"My instinct is to hold you by the hand and walk with you until we figure this out together."

She looked up at him. Her eyes flooded with hope. But Darrell shook his head.

"I won't pretend with you," he said. "When we're together and we have a problem, we'll fix it together. But this isn't *our* problem."

He leaned down and stole her lips before she could protest. She tasted bittersweet. She tasted like all of his hopes and dreams wrapped inside of a reality that needed to be worn down just a little more before it cracked and he got to the treat at the center.

When he broke the kiss, she looked at him with clear eyes. "I'm going to fix this," she said.

"Okay." He gave her low back a gentle squeeze.

"And then we'll start our life together."

"I believe in you." He pressed a kiss to her temple. "I'll be waiting."

It was the hardest thing he'd ever done in his life. Letting the woman he loved, the woman he knew with absolute certainty he'd be spending the rest of his life with, walk out the door to go back to her husband. A man who would pile problem after complaint onto her strong shoulders. A man who had come very near to breaking her.

Darrell banged his head against the closed door. His hand itched to turn the knob and chase after her. To pull her and her children out of that beast's lair and into his care.

He could do it. He could storm the castle. But he wouldn't. Beau had the strength to defeat the villain and come back to him on her own. He just needed the strength to wait for her to realize it and come back to him.

32

"Mommy, when are we gonna see Dr. Darrell again?"

Beau looked at her daughter. Flora lay on the floor of her bedroom with crayons spewed all around her and a colorful drawing before her. She drew a smile on the circular face of a stick man in a doctor's coat. Holding the stick-fingered hand of the stick doctor was a little girl with bows and a pink dress. Flora was drawing the fifth finger of a woman with long black hair and gray eyes. Beau's eyes teared at the imaginary family on the paper.

"I really liked dating Dr. Darrell," Flora said, as she finished connecting the hands of the stick-Flora to the stick-Beau. "I miss him."

Beau picked up the drawing and stared. She traced a finger down the line of the stick doctor's hands. She closed her eyes and imagined those hands embracing her, pressing into her aching back, tilting up her chin and—

"I'm not finished," Flora protested, reaching for the drawing. "I still have to draw Buck."

Beau relinquished the paper. "And your dad."

Flora frowned. "There's not enough room for Daddy." She picked up a crayon and got to work on the lines and circles that would add her brother to the picture.

Beau wished art imitated life. She wished it was that simple to shut Philip out of the picture. But in reality he'd crossed so many lines that there wasn't an eraser big enough to clean up the mess.

Darrell had accused her of pretending. But she wasn't. Philip had gotten them into a serious mess. She was trying everything she knew to get them out of it. So she could be free of her husband and get back to the man she wanted to spend the rest of her life with.

Right now, she had to stand by Philip. They were set to do a sit down interview. The camera crew had arrived and were setting up in the formal living room. Flora was dressed for a few shots with the entire family. She needed to check on her son.

Beau rose to leave Flora's room. As she passed by Buck's room, she saw him standing at the mirror, trying to tie a tie. He pulled the neck cloth wrong and huffed in frustration. She started to step into the room, but halted. His temper tantrums were usually loud and tear-stained. But he'd only given the one huff.

He took a deep breath and unballed his fists. His fingers straightened out the knot and he tried again. He worked slowly, the tip of his tongue hanging out of his mouth in concentration. After an excruciating few minutes, he got it done.

Buck turned to his mother in the doorway. His grin screamed triumph. "Look, Mommy. I did it all by myself."

His pride was infectious. Beau grinned as though he'd won the Nobel Peace Prize.

"Dr. Darrell showed me how to do it, and I did it all by myself. I didn't even ask for help."

"And you did a great job," she said. "I'm very proud of you."

"Yeah, I'm pretty good at knots. I'll go see if Flora needs any help with her shoes."

He walked past her and out of the door. She heard her children chatting amiably in Flora's room. She caught sight of Philip in the spare second floor bedroom. He pushed his arms into a blue suit coat. His hands reached up and pulled at the two ends of a tie. He fumbled for a few seconds with anxious fingers.

Beau's instinct was to offer him soothing words and then take over the tie-tying matter. But her feet held still and she watched. After fumbling for a few seconds, he threw the fabric down in a huff.

His eyes found hers in the mirror. He pointed to the discarded tie on the floor. "Can you do this for me."

Beau looked up at him. Then down at his hand. "No," she said.

Philip withdrew his hand. "What do you mean 'no'? We have to get this interview over with."

Beau shook her head. "I don't think we should do the interview. We don't need to keep up this facade of being perfect, when we're not. Let's just tell the truth."

"The truth?"

"That you made a bad decision and you're going to do everything in your power to set this right."

"Oh, I see what's going on. You're throwing me under the bus."

"I'm not throwing you. You climbed under the bus and you're trying to drag me along."

He reared back.

Beau took a deep breath. "Look, I'm not trying to abandon you. I'm going to help you. But you need to take responsibility—"

"I need to take responsibility!"

She jerked at the volume of his voice. She looked down the hallway. She wasn't sure who she was more concerned about overhearing; the kids or the television crew.

"I've done nothing but take on more and more responsibilities since the day I met you," he said. "Starting with when you got yourself knocked up."

Beau gasped as though he'd struck her.

"I've always been good to you, Beau. I've never cheated on you. I keep a roof over your head. I did this for us. The least you can do is come on camera and smile to help me make this go away."

He grabbed her upper arm and pulled her into the hallway. Beau was so shocked she came along.

"You're going to smile pretty and do this interview." His grip stayed tight as they descended the stairs.

A smile automatically spread across her face as people came into view. They sat down on the couch under the radiant lights. Philip put an arm over the back of the couch. Beau wanted to shrink away from him. But his fingers clamped down on her like a vice.

The lights glared at her. The brightness blinded her more than the darkness of her nightmares ever could. Beau tried to focus on the interviewer as she began to ask her questions.

"Mr. and Mrs. Rosen, you've been happily married for six years. We've seen you and your twins across the years. You're pillars of the community. You've built this charity that has helped so many in this city."

The interviewer looked straight at Beau. Beau opened her mouth, but nothing came out.

"The charity was originally my wife's passion," Philip filled the void. "But my love for her extended to it and then I became involved on a minor level. Beau is the brains behind everything."

He looked at her with a carnivorous smile. His light eyes filled with storm clouds. His fingers felt like thorns as they held hers.

"Is that true?" asked the interviewer. "You're the brains of the operation, Mrs. Rosen?"

Beau tore her gaze away from Philip and looked to the interviewer.

"Yes," she said. "This charity was my passion. Has always been my passion."

Beau wriggled until she was out of Philip's hold.

"I grew up fortunate," she continued. "I hate seeing people in pain, or in need. I have a habit of trying to fix the problems of others. Some would say it's a curse; that I might smother people with my good intentions and they never learn to help themselves."

She looked into Philip's eyes. They were full of wariness and confusion. Of course he wouldn't get what she was saying. It wasn't for his ears. She turned back to the cameras.

"When I heard what Yohance Stanley's firm could do, I didn't object. Too much. At first I thought it was a relief, because it's hard raising two children, managing a household, and also a business on my own."

"But you're not on your own," said the interviewer. "You have your husband."

"But as he just said, Philip has always played a minor

role in the foundation." Beau turned to him. "Isn't that right?"

She stared into crystal blue eyes. She had the faintest hope that he would step up to the plate; that he would, for once in their lives, truly take on responsibility. She was glad she didn't hold her breath.

"That's right," he said. Philip folded his hands in his lap.

Beau nodded slowly. "I didn't realize I'd made a mistake until it all came crashing down, literally. I was involved in a car crash and my doctor told me to take it easy. While I did, Mr. Stanley nearly undid all the good work the Rosen Foundation has done. I pledge now that I will be righting all of the wrongs he has caused, and then the Foundation will be dissolved."

She felt Philip stiffen beside her. "Beau—"

"That isn't the only announcement we're making tonight," she continued. "Philip and I began divorce proceedings this week. Our partnership in marriage and in business is coming to a close. Isn't that right, Philip?"

The cameras swiveled to focus on him as did the interviewer. Philip stewed. His jaw worked. But finally, he answered.

---

33

*D*arrell had thought about calling, but he knew this was the type of conversation they needed to have face-to-face. When Darrell pulled up at Beau's house the morning after her live television interview, he hadn't banked on seeing her husband. Her soon to be ex-husband he reminded himself —she'd announced they were getting a divorce on live television. She'd told the world that she was getting a divorce.

Darrell wanted to hate the man for hurting her, for dashing her dreams. But he couldn't.

Philip Rosen walked out of the door with a suitcase in his hands. He looked as though he were creeping away in the dead of night. Abandoning his family. Darrell clenched his fists.

Philip halted when he saw Darrell standing in his driveway. "I guess you're the bastard my wife's been cheating with."

The knock hit Darrell close to home. His father had left his mother for another woman. Darrell himself had had one woman cheat on him behind his back.

He wanted to open his mouth and defend what he and Beau had. What they had was true love. It couldn't compare to the farce that existed between the two of them. Darrell truly loved her, truly knew and understood her. She was better off with him. Philip didn't deserve her.

But Darrell realized there was nothing he could say, no way to defend himself. No matter what his motives were or when, exactly, it had happened, he'd fallen in love with this man's wife and, he was now and forever claiming her for his own.

Instead, Darrell asked, "Where are you going?"

Philip blinked. A moment before, he'd clearly been tensed up and ready for a confrontation; verbal, at least, if not physical. But Darrell's question gave him pause.

"What does it matter to you?" Philip said.

"It doesn't matter to me. But it will matter to your children."

"I never wanted kids."

Darrell felt the punch to his gut as though this was his own father saying these words to him. "Doesn't matter if you wanted them or not. They're here. And even if they say otherwise, they still want you."

Philip huffed and rolled his eyes.

"There's going to be another man in their lives," Darrell continued. "I'm going to be at Flora's recitals and plays. I'm going to teach Buck how to play ball and how to drive. I'm going to be there for all of the big moments and the small ones. They're going to know that they can always depend on me. But no one will ever replace their blood father."

Philip stared at him. Darrell saw give in his eyes, but then he closed them up and shrugged. The shrug was weak, as though it were unsure.

"I'm outta here," Philip called as he passed Darrell. "You can live in this fantasy land if you want."

Philip shoved the suitcase into the trunk of his car, dove inside the driver's door, and peeled out of the driveway. Darrell stared at his tire tracks before turning towards the door the other man had left open.

The house was eerily quiet in the early morning light. Darrell made his way down the hall and up the stairs. He peeked into the children's open doors. Both Buck and Flora were fast asleep. Neither of them aware that their lives were changed forever because of the tire tracks outside. Darrell stared at the twins, knowing he would do everything he could to be the father figure that they would need to successfully navigate this world.

He continued down the hall towards the master suite. He didn't knock. If she was sleeping he didn't want to wake her.

He opened the door to see Beau lying on the bed. Her hair spilled over the pillows. Darrell came in closer. She was so peaceful in her sleep, so beautiful. His heart hurt to look at her.

He leaned down and kissed her. Then he pulled back slowly. He expected to see her eyes open just like in the fairytales.

They didn't. She remained peacefully asleep.

Darrell chuckled to himself. He didn't remind himself that he didn't believe in fairytales, because he did. He'd gotten his very own storybook love. Only he knew that he and Beau were in charge of the pen. Together they would write an amazing love story every day, for the rest of their lives.

34

*B*eau slept. She slept the sleep where she knew she was dreaming, but her mind was at ease. There were no pictures playing in her mind. She was cocooned in darkness, but not an all-encompassing darkness. It felt like a warm blanket pulled over her head at dawn. There was no fear of the shadows. The only feeling was of wholeness and well being.

She felt something feather-light brush across her lips. It called her to awaken, but she wasn't ready. She craved the peace of this sleep. She didn't feel the need to chase that sensation on her lips. She somehow knew it would be there when she was ready for it. So Beau slept.

Sometime later, color washed over her mind. Her garden came into view. She heard laughter. The joyous sound of children giggling and chatting. She turned towards it. She felt herself roll over in her bed just as she turned around in her dream.

She saw her children running through the garden of her imagination. They were playing together. Flora looked happy and carefree. Buck was running behind her, a huge grin on his face. He caught up and took her hand and they ran faster through the flowers.

Beau stopped and watched them. In the distance she saw a man standing. She knew instinctively that it was Philip. But he was farther away than he'd ever been before. He turned and looked over his shoulder. He watched the children, but he didn't come any closer. His gaze connected with hers. She could feel it on her face.

She raised her hand and waved to him. All the years they'd been together; there was now a gulf between them. Philip only stared at her. Then he turned his gaze back to the children. He didn't move forward. He didn't come back. He simply turned and looked at the horizon. Beau made no move to approach him either.

At her back, Beau felt warmth. She knew who it was without looking. She felt his lips at her neck. She leaned back until the back of her head fit into the crook of his neck. He kissed her forehead, her nose, and then her lips.

Beau fell into the kiss. It called her to wakefulness, but still she wasn't ready. She stayed firmly in the peace of her dream world. Reality could wait, if this is what her mind offered her.

Darrell pulled away from her. He smiled at her. Kissed her bare, left ring finger; a promise. Before Beau could pull him closer, he took off after the children with a grin. He caught up to Flora and spun her around. He chased Buck, allowing the boy to beat him and then fall to the ground to wrestle.

In the distance, Philip stood looking out over the horizon. Darrell and her children laughed and played in the field. They looked at her, beckoning her to come and play. Beau took a step—

Her eyes opened.

The sun shone into her bedroom, lighting her face. It had all been a dream.

Was it another prophecy?

Did it really matter?

It was what her heart wanted and she'd make it happen. She would clean up this last mess that Philip had made. She would call a lawyer on Monday and start divorce proceedings. Then she'd go to Darrell a free and unencumbered woman.

Beau started at the sound of laughter coming from somewhere in the house. The clock on her side table told her that it was well into the afternoon. How had she slept so long without the kids waking her?

She slipped on a robe and headed downstairs. As she came into the living room, she noted as she went that things were clean and in order. She entered the kitchen and froze at the scene.

Buck stood on a stool with Darrell behind him. There was a spatula in his little hand as Darrell guided him into flipping a pancake. When the disc made it successfully onto the other side, Buck looked back at Darrell with a grin.

Flora was setting the table, arranging flowers in a vase. She looked up. "Hi, Mommy! We made you brunch. That's lunch and breakfast smooshed together cause you slept too long for breakfast."

"I made you the biggest pancake, Mommy," said Buck.

Beau looked at each in turn. She couldn't have imagined this scene, not in her wildest dreams. And then, like she'd wished and hoped for, Darrell's hand came to rest at the small of her back.

"Good afternoon," he said.

"How did you get in here?"

"Philip left the door open as he left."

"Daddy's gone on a trip," said Buck, as he mixed more flour into the bowl of batter. "Dr. Darrell said he's gonna stay with us while he's gone."

"Is that okay, Mommy?" asked Flora. "Can Dr. Darrell have a sleep-over?"

"I think a sleep-over would be fun," Beau said, her voice a promise.

The kids cheered.

"I thought I was supposed to be the one who came to you," she said when the kids were occupied with their duties once more.

Darrell shrugged. "I figured we could meet halfway."

She wrapped her arms around his neck. "I have to ask you a very important question, Darrell Walker."

"Yes," he said. "My answer is yes."

"You haven't heard the question."

"Doesn't matter."

"The question is," Beau hedged. "Did you clean my house?"

Darrell chuckled as he pressed his palms into her low back. "Just straightened up a little while you all slept. Hope that's okay."

"That's the sexiest thing any one's ever done for me."

"What's sexiest mean, mommy?" asked Flora.

They ate their pancakes amidst chatting and laughter. Then Darrell showed the kids how to load the dishwasher while Beau sat back and watched. Two Disney movies later and the kids were finally dozing, as dusk settled in.

Darrell scooped up Flora and bade Beau sit still until he came back for Buck. She trailed him up the stairs as he carried her sleeping little boy to bed. Her body sighed against the doorframe as he tucked Buck into his bed and pulled the sheets up under his cheek.

When he returned to her at the door, his eyes smoldered. She reached for him, but he caught her hands. "Let's talk," he said.

He led her back downstairs and into the kitchen. Going to the fridge, she produced a beer for him and a glass of wine for herself. With the glasses settled on the island, Beau caught Darrell staring at a photo on the fridge. It was a picture of her and Philip from the time when they first met.

It wasn't the first night. It was the second or third. They were at a beach house where her cousin Judas had thrown a party. She saw her brother Guy and Manny in the background. Manny and Guy were turned away from her and Philip, talking to someone who was just out of focus.

"I think that's me," Darrell said.

Beau peered down at the image. She could make out the outline of a man in a suit. A gray suit. She focused on the man's hands. She would know those hands anywhere; by sight as well as by touch.

She looked up at Darrell, her eyes wide. "It is you."

He looked at her quizzically. She reached out and pulled his head to hers, crashing their lips together. Darrell's arms came around her. The palm of his hand found the small of her back, sliding exactly where it belonged. She fit her body against his and heard a click as they fit into place.

She urged him out of the kitchen and towards the back hall. There was a guest bedroom there. He came willingly and they slipped inside.

Darrell let her go and flipped the light switch, flooding the room. "I need to see this to believe it."

Beau chuckled, but quickly turned serious. She slid her robe off. There were only two other articles of clothing to get rid of after that. The nightgown slipped over her head and her panties peeled from her hips.

The room was silent, other than Darrell's shallow breathing. He swallowed as his eyes roamed her naked body. "I'm supposed to say we should wait."

She began a slow march towards him. She had no intention of turning back. She was completely bare for him, and that included her wedding ring.

"I'd be content if you held me," she said when she reached him. "But I'd rather feel you inside of me."

His hands came around her bare body. Then his lips met hers in an all-consuming kiss. There was no more waiting. He was naked in less than sixty seconds. Before his pants hit the ground, he retrieved a foil packet.

A small wave of sadness hit as Darrell rolled the condom on. Just as the idea of being this man's life partner filled Beau with joy, the idea of parenting with this man was a dream she wanted to come true sooner rather than later. But it would have to be later.

They would lay a strong foundation before they built onto it. And that included making sure Flora and Buck had adjusted to the new make-up of their family. Right now, Darrell laid Beau out on the bed. He hovered above her, his gaze on hers.

"What?" he asked, running a hand along her body.

"You're my real dream come true," she said, as she parted her lips and then her thighs, welcoming him into her real world.

ABOUT INES JOHNSON

Lover of fairytales, folklore, and mythology, Ines Johnson spends her days reimagining the stories of old in a modern world. She writes books where damsels cause the distress, princesses wield swords, and moms save the world.

You can sign up for her mailing list and receive alerts and free reads at http://bit.ly/InesReaders.

ALSO BY INES JOHNSON
Pumpkin
Rumpeled
Beau